AMBUSH FROM ABOVE

So that's it?" Casey finally whispered.

"That's it," Jonas answered. "Pearlwood. Not many of them around."

"The tree," Casey said with the muted urgency of a mouse dashing off under a bed of leaves. "Its bark sparkles in the sunlight just like your harmonica!"

"It should," her father said without looking. "This is where I got the timber for it."

Casey frowned. Looking around again she tried to see what her father was seeing and made an important observation, or at least she thought it was important: "It's quieter here—than on the other side of the river."

"Yes," he said in a pleased tone, eyes still darting around. "Yes, it is. And the way seems suddenly darker somehow, like we're walking into an ambush."

The moment after her father said it, Casey drew a knife from her sash. By mere chance she glanced at it and saw the grisly blue face hurtling down on her from above.

Casey rolled with a shout, thrusting the knife high, and the scaly creature impaled itself with a screech and crumpled on top of her. A second later it flared brightly into blue dust.

"Cave demon!" Jonas shouted, getting to his feet and waving the noisome vapors away with both hands.

When the smoke cleared, Jonas scanned the woods.

"We're surrounded," he hissed, lifting Casey to her feet.

Looking around, Casey saw reptilian faces appearing and disappearing in the brush and peeking around trees. Then, realizing that they had been discovered, the horde began to creep closer, teeth clacking, claws flexing.

THE TAMM CHRONICLES

BOOK I

THUNDER PEAK

UPCOMMING:

BOOK II

THE GALLOPING GHOST

BOOKS BY TRAE STRATTON

TO HAVE AND TO HOLD

FOR MORE ABOUT THE AUTHOR PLEASE VISIT

WWW.TRAESTRATTON.COM

THUNDER PEAK

THE TAMM CHRONICLES
BOOK I

TRAE STRATTON

ISBN: 9798555928115 (paperback)

For Violet

THUNDER PEAK

PART I
STARFALL

1
THE SEEN AND THE UNSEEN

The rumble started low and distant.

Casey tensed, looking left and right.

Concentrating on finding the source of the steadily rolling tumult, she barely heard her friend Savannah ask, "Do you hear that? What is that?"

The oldest of their trio, Savannah's brother Nash, took off his hat, a worn Stetson with a cattleman crease handed down from his father, and looked up through the dense pines and aspens looming over them. "Might be a storm coming."

Casey focused on the trail behind them. "I don't think so."

Something was coming through the woods.

Something large.

Something fast and dangerous.

The rumble began to swell. Still looking up, Nash and Savannah covered their ears.

Darting into the nook formed by a trio of aspens, Casey tried to shout over the deafening roar racing toward them through the forest, "Look out! Look out!" But it was too late, and Casey could only watch as a stampede of horses erupted over a low hill and hurtled toward her witless friends. "No!" she screamed, fully expecting both of them to be trampled.

But they weren't.

Time slowed for Casey as she watched the herd storm through the timber at a pace more suited to the open plain. Though the herd was thirty strong at least, they didn't seem to hit anything. Not a branch, not a bush, not a leaf or even a blade of grass. It was the most amazing thing she had ever seen.

Right up until one of the rushing steeds discovered her hiding spot.

It was for the briefest possible moment, but long enough for her to see a flash of rainbow in the horse's eye when their gazes met—and the glistening silver horn on its head.

Then they were gone.

Casey stood frozen in the tree stand, incredulous that her friends were not only still alive but also oblivious to what had just happened.

Growing up in the ominous shadow of Thunder Peak, all of them were acquainted with sudden storms that seemed to arrive out of nowhere and disappear just as fast, storms that most folk living across the Arizona Territory and beyond considered tall tales.

After another few moments of stillness, Nash shrugged, looked at Savannah, and said, "I reckon that's the longest, loudest thunderclap mine ears have ever heard. And not even a drop." Then he saw Casey, breathing heavy and still backed against the sheltering aspens. "What's with you?"

"I, uh…" Casey stammered. "Didn't you see?"

"See what?" Nash asked, striding over.

Savannah picked up the hem of her blue chambray dress and closed the distance between them with sure-footed steps. "You okay?"

Casey took a deep, steadying breath. "So fast," she whispered, peering through the trees. "Come and gone in a flash."

"You saw a flash?" Savannah asked.

"Probably lightning," Nash said. "Did it hit close?"

Casey pursed her lips while an image of Old Hickory swept through her mind.

Old Hickory was an ancient Indian living in nearby Storm Town, and he told wild stories about the mountain and the forest. So wild that everyone said he was touched. Then she thought of how everyone treated Old Hickory, how they laughed at his tales of tree spirits and mysterious animals.

She laughed too because she wanted to hate Hickory. Indians had killed her mom and dad, and she wanted to hate all of them. So why she felt bad about laughing afterward was something she just couldn't understand. Times she had thought too much about it had even made her cry. And crying was stupid, so better just not to think about it.

Casey hid the thought behind making an adjustment to the long brown braid that fell down her back. Then, with no hint at what she'd really seen, Casey pointed in the direction the horses had run. "Yonder a ways."

"Let's go look," Nash said, and off they went.

They searched most of the afternoon for the place where the bolt might have hit (and Casey hunted for a hoofprint of some kind), but to no avail.

Still keeping her thoughts to herself, Casey began to question what she had seen. It was hot, and realizing it had been a while since she'd taken a sip from her leather water bag, she paused and took a long drink. Sun shadows through the trees, she decided. Sun shadows and thirst. That's what it was.

Just seemed real 'cause of the long sky rumble. That's all. Crazy to think more of it.

The fruitless search for the lightning strike continued until they reached the hilltop remains of a fallen tower who's only standing feature was a crumbling, curved wall stabbing thirty feet into the sky. The elegance of the arc suggested the fort had been sculpted like a lighthouse. A very unusual design for the West, and one that had inspired Itza Chu Canyon residents to call it Point Lookout; but its true name, along with its purpose and the identities of the people who would build such a thing in the deepest corner of a hidden valley, was just another Thunder Peak mystery.

A crisp, clear stream burbling down from the peak vanished under the rocky hill supporting the ruin, then reappeared on the opposite side and meandered away through the trees. For as long as Casey could remember, her father had issued stern warnings that the woods got much darker and dangerous on the other side of it and still made her promise every time she went exploring not to cross it.

Casey wore a long knife on a belt fastened around her buckskin pants, and Nash wore one around his dark jeans, but she knew enough about bears, mountain lions, and other wild animals to know it wouldn't be enough if it came to a fight, and so she had never broken that promise.

Alien and unique as it was, the hilltop debris field was an endless source of natural delight for Casey and her friends. Each time they explored it, they seemed to find something new and mysterious. Sometimes it was a strangely colored rock. Other times it would be a piece of pottery, a carved stone, or even a piece of steel that looked like it could have been an arrowhead, a spoon, or anything in between.

Nash was especially curious about the foundation stones. The shattered white marble blocks the tower had been constructed with were unlike anything in wood-timbered Storm Town, and while the girls looked for hidden treasures, he levered and turned the heavy stones in search of the mysterious markings he sometimes found on them. Staring hard at the chiseled lines, he would try to memorize the shapes so he could add them to the book he was making back home.

As interesting as the symbols were, what fascinated Casey most was a small window near the very top of the crumbling wall that had miraculously survived whatever had befallen the tower.

A window full of color.

Eager to know more, then eleven-year-old Casey had asked her teacher if she'd ever seen a colored window and was told that many churches had them, especially in Europe. They were called stained glass windows and often held pictures that told stories.

Wondering what its story might be, Casey had looked up at that unreachable window for years.

Then, in the spring of 1885, Casey turned fourteen, ushering in a sudden, thrilling change. The planting season had kept them all away from the site for months, but with the summer came some free time, and when she returned, the picture glass no longer seemed as unattainable as it used to be.

Staring up at the window, Casey gritted her teeth. The six previous attempts she'd made through the long hot summer had met with varying degrees of success, some getting her closer, some ending in abject failure.

Abject failure defined by scrapes, cuts, sprains, and other hurts.

"Let it be, Casey." Savannah cut into her thoughts. "Before your stubbornness cracks your head and turns you into worm food."

Casey pulled her eyes from the window to peer at Savannah, three years her junior.

"Oh, I know that look like a bee knows honey," Savannah shook her dark curls. "Nash! You better get over here and help me talk some sense into Casey before she goes for her angel wings again."

Nash huffed and looked over at them. "C'mon Casey," he said. "Last time you twisted your ankle. Time before that your whole hand swelled up. Time before that you lost your grip and skinned both your arms sliding down. Savannah's right. What's it going to take?"

"I just." Casey's voice fell away as she looked back up at the window. "I just want to see it."

"It's probably nothing," Nash said. "A trick of the light."

"No." Casey shook her head with certainty. "No way. It's a picture glass."

"All right, so it's a picture glass," Savannah threw her hands in the air. "What difference will it make? You can't take it with you."

"I don't *want* to take it with me." Casey's eyes grew wide with exasperation. "I just want to *see* what the picture *is*."

Nash followed Casey's gaze. "What we need," he said as the answer dawned on him, "is a rope! Next time we'll bring a rope, and I'll hold it down on the other side while you climb up."

"Shiny idea!" Savannah exclaimed. "A rope. For next time."

"Shiny swell," Casey said, nodding in agreement. "So good we should have thought of it long before now. But…" Casey's voice faded.

"But what?" Nash asked. "It's the best thing for it."

Casey shrugged her shoulders. "A rope feels like cheating. I don't want to mizzle out."

"Mizzle out!" Savannah cried. "You done tried enough times that courage got nothing to do with it."

"Savannah's right," Nash said evenly. "If anyone's gone and mizzled out, it's me, a long time ago. But that's no bother. I asked my pa and he told me, 'Courage in the heart gets a body kilt what got no smarts behind the eyes.'"

"You're right," Casey said. "You're both right. But I want to do it. I have to try one more time."

"Nothing but a sack of flusteration—that's what you are, Casey Tamm." Nash waved his hand at her. "Good luck, then."

Casey's eyes fled from the window to find Nash's back as he walked away. The sight of it opened a pit in her stomach she didn't quite understand.

"Nash, wait." Casey's voice brought his head around, and she flashed a smile that made him pause. "Last time, okay? If I don't make it, I'll wait until we get a rope to try again. I promise. Don't leave."

Nash sighed. "You just want me here to carry you again if you get hurt."

Casey looked up at the window and smiled again, this time to herself. Nash had insisted on carrying her the day she hurt her ankle. About halfway home she knew her leg was fine but found being in his arms too surprisingly delightful to have him set her down. She couldn't tell him that, of course. That thought was scarier than climbing up to the window.

"Would that?" Casey stammered suddenly. "I mean, is that so bad? If I wanted, not if you don't want to."

They locked eyes for a long moment. Then a change came over Nash, and he shook his head. "All right. Last time, though. You promised."

"I did. I do." She nodded quickly, and deciding it was best to stop talking, Casey sent him another smile.

Then she was off, dancing from stone to stone through the long-stemmed garnet and gold blooms that only grew around this particular hill, eyes darting over the wall, trying to find enough handholds to get her to the window. Her starting point chosen, Casey wasted not an instant on second thoughts and began to scurry up.

Wait a minute, she thought, whirling around to look back at the flowers now ten feet below her. *This is where we were. The day Dad told me about…*

Casey's back stiffened.

Eyes peering suddenly into the past, she fell completely in thrall to an unlocking memory.

How no one can explain why the flower petals here change colors every morning. And if I ever saw something as unique as these flowers…

So deep in memory was Casey that her left hand slipped free, but before the danger could snap her away, some distant part of her mind told her not to worry. That she could still hold on. Because this was more important than falling.

Important…

Casey stared at the flowers, dangling by one hand.

The horses…were not just horses. They were invisible horses—with horns! Not sun shadows…and not crazy!

"Unique!" Casey laughed out loud and abruptly broke the memory spell with the sound of her own voice.

Stunned by the sudden realization that she was hanging by one hand, Casey twisted back around in a panic and mashed her nose into the wall. Ignoring the blood running into her mouth, Casey spotted a decaying seam in easy reach. Her left hand darted out, but before she could grasp it, the crack she clung to with her right broke away under her weight and she fell.

Casey landed with a grunt amid the flowers below. Distantly she heard Nash and Savannah shouting as they raced over.

She lay still, as if dead, her eyes focused on a flower just inches from her aching nose.

Her heart was pounding. Pounding on the door holding back the rest of the memory until finally it splintered and shattered.

Casey had been adopted by her father as an infant. Long ago, when he took her to the tower for the very first time, he promised that if she ever saw something as unique as the flowers growing there, he would tell her a secret about her parents.

"Casey!" a voice called, but she wasn't ready yet.

Beset by the intrigue of it all, she had tried many times to trick him, but her father was sharp as a tack and always seemed to have an explanation about her discoveries—and could tell when she was fibbing. And those fibs had been punished severely with extra chores until eventually she gave up trying to trick him. Shortly after that she stopped searching too.

"Casey!" the voice called again.

That was all years ago, before she'd even turned ten, and something she had nearly forgotten.

Casey's eyes lit up.

Nearly, not completely.

"Casey!" a smaller voice pleaded, and a tremble went through her body, replacing the window and everything else she knew with one desire: to get home as fast as she could and speak to her father. To tell him all about the invisible horses with horns on their heads and find out what he knew about her parents.

"Casey!" Nash shook her again. "Can you hear me? Can you move?"

"Yeah." Casey shook her head, clearing away the last of the memories. "Yeah, I'm all right." She sat up slowly. "Just a little…dazed."

Nash was on his knees and sat back on his heels, eyes wild.

"That was," he said, shaking his head. "That was—"

"The scariest thing I've ever seen in my life," Savannah exclaimed. "Eyes open and empty like a dead body! You're a durn fool, Casey Tamm. Serve you right to be kilt right now!"

Casey nodded. "I am a durn fool, Savannah. I am, and I'm sorry for scaring you. Both of you."

Casey tried to smile at Nash, but his face was frozen, as if he were looking at a ghost.

"Your rope idea is the ticket." Casey stood and looked over at Savannah. "With a rope, we might be able to get you up for a look too."

The younger girl just stared back at her, eyes wide.

"Your face is all bloody," Nash said, getting to his own feet. "You sure you're all right?"

Casey wiped her face on her sleeve, wincing when she touched her nose. "I'll be fine. What do you say, Savannah? You want to have a look too?"

Mollified by the quick cleanup, Savannah brightened slightly. Then she smiled up at the window with fresh wonder. "Seeing as you're all right, I can cotton to that!"

"Next time, with a rope, like I promised," Casey added, looking at Nash, who gave her a weak nod and an even weaker smile.

"Well, I'm for heading home," she continued. "How 'bout you, Savannah?"

"Dinner bell be ringing soon enough," Savannah agreed.

Though Nash was the oldest at fifteen and the de facto leader of their group, he had grown accustomed to yielding to Casey, who everyone agreed evinced a surprising amount of clarity and maturity for her age.

"Reckon you two are right," Nash said, glancing around with a disappointed frown. "All right. Let's head back."

"Don't forget to grab some flowers for your ma," Casey added, plucking one and placing it in her hair.

"Oh yeah." Nash's eyes lit up. "Thanks for reminding me."

Hidden in the foliage across the stream, a pair of topaz eyes watched the trio turn and head away. They blinked once, glittering like gemstones, and then disappeared as if they had never been.

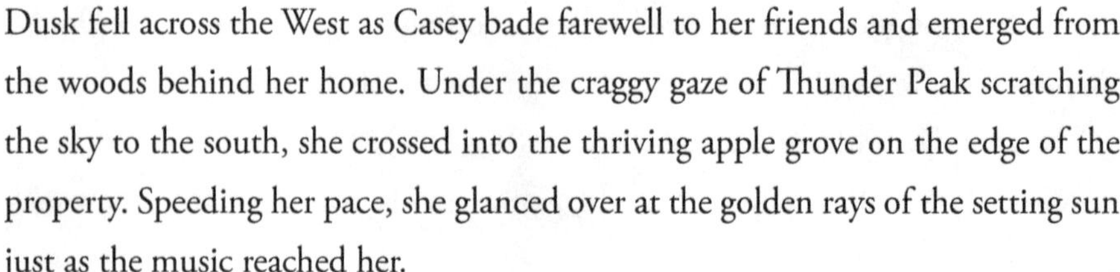

Dusk fell across the West as Casey bade farewell to her friends and emerged from the woods behind her home. Under the craggy gaze of Thunder Peak scratching the sky to the south, she crossed into the thriving apple grove on the edge of the property. Speeding her pace, she glanced over at the golden rays of the setting sun just as the music reached her.

That would be her father, on the front porch, mesmerizing the sunthorns with his pearlwood harmonica.

Casey smiled at the sturdy dwelling she had called home for as long as she could remember. With its stone foundation and wooden second story, it was bigger and sturdier than what anyone else had bothered to build in the valley. She and her father lived alone, but they had descended from a large family of ranchers in Texas with lots of money.

Wealth enough to let her father, Jonas, meander off deeper into the West, where he discovered Storm Town, and to buy up an abandoned homestead, a place to heal his heart after his wife and son died during childbirth. Several years later, when Jonas's brother and his wife were killed in an Indian attack on their stagecoach, it was the only moment of joy he'd known since he'd left when he was asked to adopt little Casey, who had miraculously survived the raid nestled in a woven basket.

Fourteen years later it was an arrangement that had worked out for everyone. Casey had been an infant when her parents died and knew only one father, and that was Jonas. To her the picture of her natural parents on the fireplace mantle held strangers, but their gazes were warm, and it was comforting to know they had loved her and that Jonas had welcomed her as his own with an open heart.

They got by comfortably with a few animals and the money they made from the apples they sold or traded. Apples that everyone said were the best they'd ever tasted and were willing to pay extra for. No one could figure out why they were so big and red and juicy, or why they grew and ripened so fast.

When pressed, her father always chuckled the kind of chuckle that made you wonder, saying it must be something natural in the soil or the quirky cloud-free rainstorms the area was famous for.

The truth might be debatable, but there was one hard fact that was not:

Tamm Ranch and Orchard had become part of the Thunder Peak legend. A very profitable part of the legend.

What it all meant for Casey was that she grew up happy and content. That is, except for one troubling, nearly forgotten secret. A secret she was positive was about to be revealed.

Tingling with excitement, Casey reached the porch and quietly struck the mud and dirt from her moccasins before clambering up the worn wooden steps. Just as she had suspected, her father was rocking gently in the porch swing.

With his bare feet perched on the rail, the white bark harmonica he'd made himself gliding back and forth over his lips, and his dusty hat pulled low against the ebbing sun, Jonas Tamm, much like the pioneers, Indian fighters, law men, and outlaws who defined the age, had evolved beyond *who* he was or *what* he'd done. Properly defined, he didn't just *live* on the frontier; he was a *part* of the West that people living in places like New York, Boston, and Philadelphia read about in newspapers and dime-store novels.

Growing up in a hidden valley on the southern edge of the Arizona Territory, that was all lost on Casey, at least for now. To her, there was something comforting about seeing her father in the swing, and it always made her smile.

Similar to honeybees, but thrice again larger, sunthorns were dangerous insects when aroused and, as their name suggested, glowed with golden luminescence. They came out at dusk, buzzing down out of the dense woods surrounding Thunder Peak, using their light to attract and feed on other, smaller night insects. Despite their fierce demeanor, they evinced an inexplicably playful fascination with music. Just now her father had a shimmering cloud of dozens over his head, roiling and twirling in the twilight to the haunting melodies of his harmonica.

Casey sat beside him, and her father spared a quick glance to wink at her. She smiled, and then, despite all the desperate excitement bubbling up inside her to blurt out what had happened in the woods, she forced herself to calm down and open up to the nuances of the music.

After a while Casey began to hum and sway. Finally, she began to sing and slowly took over the tune, sending the "sunnies" racing high and low through the evening sky with the tempo and timbre of her song.

Then it was her father's turn to sit back, hypnotized, as Casey coaxed the sunthorns to weave their glow with the rays of the setting sun into a flashing tapestry of dancing lights that enveloped the entire front of their house.

After urging the sunnies through a final crescendo that melted into the sunset, Casey let her voice trickle down to a somber low that gently disappeared with the last light of the day and released the insects to find their dinner.

"That was amazing Nightingale," her father said, using the nickname he had given her because of her singing voice. "One of your best efforts yet."

Casey finished catching her breath and then flashed a mischievous smile. "Not as amazing as what I saw today in the woods with Savannah and Nash."

"Really?" her father said, seeing the dried blood on his daughter's face and the flower tucked in her ear for the first time. "What happened to your nose?"

"I fell." Casey waved her hand. "I'm fine."

"Climbing again?" Jonas asked.

"Climbing again." Casey nodded, and Jonas noticed her toes tapping with impatience.

"Right then, sounds like a great dinner story. Let's go."

Jonas watched Casey jump off the swing and run inside. Rising after he heard the door close, Jonas placed his hands on the rail and gazed after the sunthorns disappearing into the night. When the last of them had gone, he took a deep breath and then another to quell the stomach flips that came with seeing a dragon eye daisy tucked behind Casey's ear. Vigorously rubbing his cheeks, he tried to etch a passable smile on his face, and only when he was sure that he'd done so did he turn and follow his daughter inside.

"I'm still not sure why Nash and Savannah didn't see the horses, but once we reached Point Lookout, I remembered what you told me about Old Hickory. About how maybe some of his stories aren't as crazy as they sound, and that one day, maybe, animals that no one has seen in a long time may come back. And if they did, and I ever saw one, or something else that couldn't be explained, you would tell me a secret about my parents that would explain it. That's what happened, right? Something unique, like the flowers by Point Lookout? Something that can't be explained? Please tell me already—why aren't you saying anything?"

Having risen out of her chair several times to dramatically reenact the events of the afternoon, Casey had hardly touched her food.

Jonas looked at his own plate and forced down another mouthful. *She's only fourteen*, he thought sadly. *I thought I would have more time.* The moment he thought it, however, Jonas knew it was a lie. The truth was, he had given up hope and figured he had the rest of their lives to come clean.

Jonas put his fork down and wiped his mouth. He had only lied to Casey once, out of necessity, about her origins. Ready or not, it was time to tell her the truth.

Today.

Now.

Jonas sighed inwardly. Somewhere through the years the "ready or not" part had begun to say more about him than Casey. For both their sakes, he would have to break the news like he would break a new colt. Slow and steady.

“First.” Jonas began, looking Casey in the eye, “I’ve been waiting for you to say all you had to say.”

Casey rolled her eyes but knew that was a test and remained quiet.

“Impressive,” her father said with a smirk. “You’re growing up. That one always used to get you.”

Casey smiled back whimsically but still said nothing.

“Right then, second. Pick up your fork and start eating. I’m going to refill our glasses, and when half your plate is empty, it’ll be my turn to talk and tell you that they were more than just horses. That they were from your mother’s homeland. What that all really means and everything else you want to know.”

Jonas’s eye wandered to the portrait on the mantle. *And maybe a few things you don’t—not really.*

Casey’s meadow-green eyes gleamed with delight and she began eating as fast as she could. Jonas smiled, and on his way to retrieve the water pitcher, couldn’t resist tousling the long walnut braid hanging down her back. He topped her glass first, then refilled his own and quickly drained it. *What I really need is a beer*, he thought.

Jonas refilled his glass a second time and was about to sit down when a galloping horse reared to a halt outside. Loud steps pounded up the porch, and a heavy hand pelted the door.

“Jonas!” someone called. “Jonas!”

Jonas did not answer.

The Arizona Territory of the mid-1880s was a dangerous land prowled by Geronimo and countless outlaws. While growing up in Texas, Jonas had learned all about planning ahead from his father and then saw its benefits in action while serving in the Confederate Army. As a result, all it took was one simple, silent nod to his daughter for the pair to quietly take positions of readiness to deal with hostile strangers.

Jonas padded to the coat rack, put on his gun belt, and pulled his pistol.

"Jonas!" the voice called again, followed by more banging.

Stepping up beside the door, not in front of it, he looked back to check that Casey had armed herself with her own pistol and taken cover. Another nod to her, and then he called out, "Who is it?"

The answer came quick and breathless. "It's me Hob, Jonas. Hob Watkins."

The window closest to the door had been configured horizontally at shoulder height, wide enough to let in plenty of light but high enough to prevent someone, or something, from barreling through.

Jonas peered out, and the first thing he noticed was the star on Hob's vest. "That's right." Hob nodded, looking up at him. "Deputy Hob tonight."

Jonas opened the door, and Hob continued, "Trouble, Jonas. Lots of it. Sheriff Tanner asked me to come see if he could count on you and your rifle, usual like."

Jonas nodded. "Of course, Hob. We have to protect our own. Tell the sheriff I'll ride out as soon as I can."

Hob smiled, obviously relieved, and then grimly handed him a deputy shield of his own.

Jonas took it, gave him a quick nod, and closed the door. When Hob's steps receded, he turned to face his daughter. Casey was staring back at him with a resigned look in her eyes.

Jonas gestured for her to sit back down at the table and finish her meal, then sat down beside her. "Looks like I have some work to do."

This was far from the first time her father had been summoned by the sheriff. Casey nodded and then looked up at him. "Bad people come to Storm Town again?"

"Sounds like it, yes." Jonas put his hand on her shoulder. "I want you to stay here and practice your words and numbers. Just like always. If I'm not home in the morning, do not start your chores. You do not go out at all until I return. If I can't get back by nightfall, I'll send word to Widow Dorn to come fetch you. That door opens for nobody else."

Casey nodded.

"And don't worry. We'll pick up talking where we left off as soon as I get back."

"Promise?" Casey asked.

"Promise," her father replied.

She gave him another satisfied nod, shuffled over to put her gun away, and then resumed her meal while he went upstairs to prepare.

On the inside Casey was struck not only by utter disappointment, but the chilly fingers of trepidation that accompanied those days when the sheriff needed her father's help. Riding into Storm Town looking for trouble was dangerous, without a doubt; but at the same time, it was more than that.

It meant the *change* was coming.

The transformation was heralded by a unique sound all its own, and for as long as she could remember, the sinister jangle that meant her father had pinned the star on set her on edge and filled her with a sense of foreboding.

Casey could only wait for it, staring at her plate as the minutes plodded along.

Playing with her food.

Waiting, until—without preamble the first eerie *thump-cliinz* of boot and spur struck the stairs and slid into the base of her neck like a frozen thorn.

The hateful sound moved through her like venom, weakening all her muscles right down to her suddenly tingling toes.

Thump-cliinz, thump-cliinz.

Casey winced at every spur-laden step.

Thump-cliinz, thump-cliinz.

Each footfall sending another icy chill down her spine.

Lost somewhere deep down, Casey knew how she felt was silly, that all the men wore spurs. That she might have to wear them too one day if her dream of being a real-life lady marshal came true.

Thump-cliinz, thump-cliinz.

But the dire sense of foreboding in that horrible sound just wouldn't let her catch that common-sense thought so she could get passed it.

Finally he reached the floor, and Casey took a deep, steadying breath, knowing that when she looked up, it wouldn't just be his footwear that had changed. It would be everything.

And so it was.

Gone were the worn woolen trousers, red flannel shirt, and gray vest; in their place were brown jeans, a dark shirt, and a long black duster that fell beyond his knees. On his head was a creased, starless-night-colored Stetson that he only wore when the sheriff called for him.

Dressed as he was now, gathering his guns to the spectral cadence of heavy boot steps and spinning spurs, her father seemed to Casey a ghost of the man he had been just minutes ago, let alone the barefoot man waiting for her on the porch. Before long he was standing by the door, and without his asking, Casey went over and gave him a long hug.

As always, Jonas misinterpreted her expression and kissed the top of her head. "Don't worry, Nightingale," he said, nestling the thick braid over her front shoulder and smoothing it down. "I'll be fine." Then, after a quick wink and a warm smile, he closed the door behind him.

Jonas waited for the bolts on the other side of the door to slide home. Once they did he kissed his fingers and pressed them gently against the heavy door.

Taking a deep breath, he headed for the stable, and by the time he had saddled his horse and begun riding for Storm Town, there was a different, unsettling manner to his bearing—a gait and glance that suited his new attire. An edge in his eyes that folk living west of the Mississippi would recognize immediately as windows to a soul best left unseen.

A soul full of darkness.

And it was for that darkness, which Jonas could unleash from one cold, steady eye into the barrel of a rifle and deliver with gunpowder and lead as fast and accurate as anyone who ever held a bullet, that he had been called on by the sheriff.

Death's Breath.

That's what they had called him during the War Between The States, and it was a side of him that Jonas hoped Casey would never have to see.

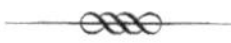

Casey sat at the table long after her father had left, eating slowly, gazing far away, trying to forget the look of him as he walked out the door by musing on what little he had revealed before Hob had come to deputize him.

From your mother's homeland, her father had said.

What did *that* mean? Was she from another country?

More than just horses.

And what *could* that mean? And how was it that her father knew? To Casey, it sounded an awful lot like a secret that should have passed on with her mother.

More than just horses.

As a kid she had never really thought it through, figuring the secret was just something she would learn some day and continue on after having learned it. But it was completely and utterly different now that she had really, truly seen something that couldn't be explained: a horse with a horn.

A silver horn.

The secret must be bigger than she ever imagined.

So big that even after she had seen something that made her father agree to tell her what it was, she still couldn't even put new questions to it.

Casey reached into her blouse and pulled out the silver pendant she wore around her neck. It was molded in the shape of a flying hawk with a wingspan over three inches across.

The craftsmanship was meticulous, rife with masterful strokes that showed individual feathers. However, Casey thought its most striking feature was the green turquoise stones embedded in the hawk's wings and eyes. Despite the charm's weight, the brown leather braid that held it showed no signs of fraying, even after years and years of wear.

The talisman had been her mother's.

Jonas claimed it after taking Casey in and wore it in memory of his brother and his wife, and as a reminder of how important the responsibility of being Casey's new father was.

Then, on her tenth birthday, he had surprised Casey by gifting it to her, saying it was more important now that she have something by which to remember them, especially her mother.

And she had worn it every day since.

Casey let out a long breath and tucked the pendant back into her shirt. There was nothing for it. Best to keep her mind busy, like her father had said.

Casey walked over to the bookshelf and began reading through the titles of their books and paperbacks: *McGuffey's Eclectic Primer, The American Women's Home*…

"Ugh," Casey mumbled. "None of that tonight. I need a story."

The Legend of Sleepy Hollow; Monowano, The Shawnee Spy; The White Wizard; Hawk-eye the Hunter; Moby Dick; The Frontier Angel; Malaeska, Indian Wife of the White Hunter; The Seminole Chief…

"*Alice's Adventures in Wonderland*," Casey murmured, pulling the book into her hands. "Here we go. Only read you once—"

Ahhwoooooo-wwoooo-wwooo.

A new, different kind of chill fingered Casey's spine, shaking her body so suddenly, so violently that she dropped the book and glanced at the door.

She didn't often hear the wolves that dwelled in the dark woods beyond Point Lookout, but every time she did, their howls made her heart race.

Though wolves were of course common in the West, and most everyone harbored a healthy, fear-laden respect for them, Casey's response was more acute and emotional. Far worse than the unease she felt around spurs. Nightmares about red-eyed wolves snapping and growling at her from the shadows had plagued her for years, and though the dreams had subsided some time ago, mountain howls still made her feel defenseless and afraid.

Ahhwoooooo-wwoooo-wwooo.

Actually—Casey calmed herself by clutching the hawk pendant—*now that I think on it, the dreams went away when Dad gave me this. He said that proved it was good luck. But maybe it's something else. Maybe it's part of the secret!*

More she didn't know. What she did know, from experience, was that once the wolves scented human settlements, their howls routinely faded away, back into the darker corners of Thunder Peak Wood, and this time was no different.

For a little while.

2
DANGERS IN THE NIGHT

Jonas peered up and down First Street from his perch atop Jack Wall's Leather Goods. From there he could clearly see up and down the lane in both directions, and the front of the Aces High Saloon.

The entire West was rife with rustlers, so the brave rancher who had identified the men in town that night as having stolen a dozen head of cattle last month had to be defended for the benefit of all. Purportedly, the gang was loosely organized, but with federal troops pressed into conflict with Geronimo, they were utilizing sheer numbers to intimidate local lawmen and growing in notoriety throughout the area, rustling livestock, robbing banks, and raiding trains with impunity.

Tanner had informed him when he arrived at the sheriff's office that over the past few months at least three or four posses had ridden through looking for an outfit calling itself the Red Ridge Riders. The gang was dug in on a sheltered plateau in another arm of the canyon that was all but unassailable, and so each party had given up and gone home. Now they were Storm Town's problem.

Nestled in a shrouded valley along the southwestern edge of the Chiricahua Mountains that the Apache had named Itza Chu Canyon, Storm Town was an outlier, even for the West. Comprised of less than thirty buildings and homes—some of those abandoned—it boasted no post office or telegraph. Down as they were near the Mexican border, Jonas supposed it wasn't even on a map, so if any of the rustlers had ever even heard of it, it had probably been through a ghost story.

Unfortunately, in holding their position, the outlaws must have realized the whole valley was inhabited by just a couple hundred or so residents with a town-nominated sheriff and a single deputy, and the temptation of what seemed to be an easy target had since dispelled the unease around any spooky legends they'd been told.

Storm Town's origin began in the 1830s with a bank robber named Black Blake Farrington. Blake, his girlfriend, Arlene, and several other thieves they worked with discovered a lush, hidden valley beneath a nameless mesa while trying to lie low after a big score. That night, when they made camp, Arlene whispered to Blake she was pregnant. Right then and there, Blake said he was giving up crime and building her a house with his own two hands. And he did. Luckily, Blake had unwittingly chosen an area flush with hidden springs perfectly suited for well water, a temperate, geological marvel that was also rampant with wildlife and greenery.

After helping the couple cut trees and get a roof over their head, their partners bid farewell and moved off. Over time, however, they started coming back, one by one, with wives of their own, and building their own small houses. Gradually, former associates of Blake's partners began to show up, many of them just intending to camp out while search parties scoured the mountains for them. The smarter ones returned later, ready to give up the way of the gun and imbue the town with another skill communities needed to survive such as farming, carpentry, blacksmithing, laundering, tailoring, boot-making, and the like.

So it was, nearly ten years after Blake Farrington had built the first house, that a man named Timothy Tocchet, who everyone called Tricky Tim because of his sleight of hand, built and opened up a saloon.

Rumor had it that the day it was finished, Tricky Tim was contemplating a blank sign with a paintbrush in his hand when a clap of thunder boomed over his head.

Tricky Tim looked up and though he didn't see a cloud in the sky, wrote Storm Town Saloon on the sign and hung it up. Tricky Tim got sick a few years later and held a poker tournament to see who would inherit the place. Ford Holis won the legendary tournament with four of a kind—aces of course. Everyone called him Ace Holis after that, and he renamed the establishment Aces High.

Despite the name change of its first saloon, the name Storm Town stuck. Given its residents—some might say because of them—the community thrived in isolation, utilizing a strong barter system that began with Blake and his original partners. Ironically, over half a century later, and in a town established by thieves no less, goods were still worth more than money in Storm Town.

The events that had put Jonas on the roof with a rifle were a perfect example. He himself traded regularly with the rancher who had been robbed, as did everyone else living in the vicinity. So losing the cattle didn't just hurt the rancher; it meant less beef and milk for everyone he bartered with too.

Property, therefore, was looked after as fiercely as in any town in the country by residents who knew a thing or two about frontier justice. Fortunately, the man actually appointed to that task was good at it, and the need to summon his standby deputies arose rarely.

That man, Sheriff Walt Tanner, along with his regular deputy, Jim Jenson, and his front-line appointees, Hob Watkins and Jesse Mills, waited for the perpetrators in the street. Unless trouble broke out inside the saloon, they planned to confront the rustlers when they emerged and offer them a chance to surrender peacefully and stand trial.

If they didn't take it, the shooting would start.

Back when Jonas had first arrived and settled in Storm Town, Sheriff Tanner's recruitment speech had been simple and blunt: "The law doesn't need fair fights in Storm Town, Jonas; it needs to be upheld. Now I know a soldier when I see one, and I can tell that you and that rifle of yours will go a long way toward making sure that happens."

Tonight that was Jonas's job. To uphold the law from a rooftop with a rifle. If need be, that included killing as many men as needed killing before they could do any more harm to his friends and neighbors.

Last thing anyone in the valley needed was for the Red Ridge Riders or any other active gang to make Storm Town a regular watering hole. Sheriff Tanner had put it best and won him over when he had noted, "Make no mistake. Spooky legends and ghost stories aside, every time you and your rifle, and any other gun, lends a hand to uphold the law, word gets 'round to those needs hearing it. Word that keeps those unable to change their ways moving on to Tombstone or Tucson. Word that keeps this town, our town, and everyone who depends on it safe and quiet like."

There was no arguing the sheriff's wisdom in that now. After all, nearly twenty years later, the close-knit town was doing well enough and still growing occasionally, albeit very slowly. More importantly, both he and Tanner were on into their forties and still alive.

Being on the roof always reminded Jonas of the war. Jensen had asked him about it once, but Tanner cut him off. "War's over son," he said. "Don't matter who did what for who. We're one country again, and all's forgiven. Lincoln said so himself, and no one in Washington's ever said any different."

Jonas wondered if Tanner would feel the same way if he knew the truth about his rifleman on the roof and what he'd done during those awful years. Jonas glanced down at Liberty. Liberty was a Sharps Model 1859 that he'd recovered from a Northern scout who had seemingly died of pneumonia or some other disease while on an unknown mission. The dead scout, or some other previous owner, had carved a bell into the stock. Looking at it reminded him of a rendering of the Liberty Bell he'd seen in a newspaper once. Hence the name he'd given it: Liberty.

As far as Jonas was concerned, Liberty had saved his life. Though he was a natural-born shootist, it was a miracle he had survived as long as he had using the lousy weapons the South had been fighting with. Armed with the breech-loading Liberty he had become a sniper—a sharpshooter, as it were—taking to the trees and felling the enemy from a distance.

During the Seven Days' Battles in Virginia, a fellow soldier said he would have been killed twice over if the Yankee he'd been fighting hadn't unexpectedly fallen over dead like they'd been kissed by death's own breath. Several others claimed to have had the same thing happen to them, and just like that, the name stuck. Good thing for Jonas too, because depending on your colors, the name Death's Breath was still growing in fame and notoriety when the war ended. So much so that two decades later there were still many bitter Northerners who would pull pistols on any man they crossed trails with claiming to be Death's Breath, and having his real name fall into disuse protected his identity from anyone still holding a grudge.

Deep down Jonas didn't really blame them. As the war dragged on, he'd begun to question if he was on the right side of it. His family had too. By the time Jonas returned home, he was happy to discover that his father had sold their cotton fields and gone into ranching.

Jonas shook his head, set those thoughts aside and turned his mind to Casey. He should be worrying about the future, not the past. On the ride to town, Jonas had begun to dread telling her the truth, or at least admitting that he had lied to her all these years about her ma and pa. She was the most important thing in the world to him, and he didn't want to lose her trust. Truths like these were dangerous stones hidden under the road. Once time and circumstance brought about the right amount of rain and mud to bring them to the surface, it didn't matter how well built the wagon was. The wheels that drove it could always shatter.

Jonas drew a long, quiet breath and then took a small drink from his canteen. After readjusting his hat, he fixed his eyes back on the door across the street and set about once again finding the words he would tell Casey, the words he would use to explain the how and whys of the situation, when the swinging door across the street slammed open and several men came tumbling out, laughing and cursing.

"Evening, boys." Sheriff Tanner's voice rose up into the night.

Jonas quietly inhaled and exhaled through his nose, expanding his lungs. Then, sighting a straight line between the long barrel of his Sharps rifle and the chest of one of the rustlers, he whispered the words his father had taught him many years ago: "First your heart, then your hands."

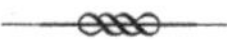

Reading by lamplight always made Casey drowsy. Despite the magnitude of the day's events, she eventually succumbed to weariness and snuggled into the couch with a cozy blanket. She had just blown out the lamp and settled in, pulling her knees up close and praying for her father, when there was a strange noise outside.

Clump-clump-clump.

Casey's eyes snapped open. *That couldn't have been as close as it sounded,* she thought. The seconds marched away while Casey lay on the couch, still as a rock, listening. Just as she was ready to believe that danger had come and gone, or perhaps never visited at all, the sound came again.

Clump-clump-clump.

Heavy footsteps. A bear maybe, sniffing around for scraps. No problem. She was safe inside with the doors locked.

Ahhwoooooo-wwoooo-wwooo.

Casey jumped, then slid off the couch and skittered toward the secret wall socket where the weapons and ammunition were stored.

Ahhwoooooo-wwoooo-wwooo!

Pacing through familiar steps, Casey should have found her way easily through the dark.

But not tonight.

Not with her thoughts rolling like a boulder down a steep hill: *Wolves! Not bears! And close! Too close! Why aren't they turning back? Nothing ever comes this close. It's like they know I'm here alone!*

Casey stumbled to the wall panel, struggled to open it, and finally retrieved the converted 1851 Colt Navy her father had given her.

A heavy, probing thud struck the front door, and Casey looked up in alarm—just in time to see the door shudder under another heavy thump.

Heart screaming in her chest, Casey burst into a sudden sweat.

That ain't no wolf!

Then bullet after bullet slipped through her fingers as she tried to load her pistol. For every bullet chambered, at least three fell and rolled away across the timbered floor.

There was another thud and then a fourth before a paralyzing, bloodthirsty wail rent the air, so loud it shook the windows. So close it seemed to be inside the house with her!

Ahhwoooooo-wwoooo-rrrrr!

Casey finished loading the gun at last and sat next to the ammunition on the floor with her back to the wall. She held the pistol up with both hands, but still it trembled, wavering in the direction of the door.

Then she heard her father's voice: "Control your breathing. You won't hit anything if everything is shaking. Remember: First your heart, then your hands."

"First your heart, then your hands," she whispered to herself. "First your heart—"

Rrrrrrrr-grrrrr-urrrrr!

The frightening growl was followed by the most jarring sounds Casey had ever heard, and she winced through an endless minute of yowling, snapping, barking, and heavy, scuffling steps—scratch-slide-scritch and clump-clump-clumpaclump—with her pistol aimed at the door.

Then an angry, piercing neigh rose unexpectedly above the growling, making her fear for the horses and other animals in the barn. The thought of them being torn apart brought hot tears to her eyes, and the gun that had begun to sag in her hands rose up again with renewed determination.

Finally there was rib-smashing whump, and something heavy fell to the ground. A miserable whine-yowl that was agony to the ear filled the air. A moment later it was cut short by a stomach twisting clump-clumpclump-*thlump*!

Silence ensued, and Casey waited in the still darkness of the house for what might happen next, the blackness swallowing her whispers even as they left her lips. "First your heart, then your hands. First your heart, then your hands." But the hollow void of the aftermath of whatever had happened lingered and lingered until the gun drooped uneasily into Casey's lap and she closed her eyes.

"Hello…"

Casey gasped and brought up the pistol. "First your heart, then your hands. First your heart, then your hands."

"Is someone in there?"

"First your heart—"

"Can anyone hear me?"

The voice in her head was laced with so much despair it descended upon Casey with palpable weight. Her heart slowed of its own accord, and then she heard herself whisper, "I can hear you."

"I can almost feel you…like the scent of a flower on the wind that comes and goes. If you can hear me…"

"I can hear you," Casey said again, this time a little louder.

"Please…"

Casey shook her head to clear it. *What am I doing? Am I dreaming? First seeing crazy things, and now hearing crazy things? I'm turning into Hickory.*

The voice came again: "I am…injured…"

No. Dad didn't think I was crazy. He knows I saw something and knows what it is. This is real.

Casey stood, almost against her will, and moved slowly through the dark toward the door. Stopping a few paces away, she stared at it. Seemingly, whatever was talking to her was right outside and needed her help. *No*—she corrected herself—*it* is *outside*. She knew it.

But did it really need her help, or was it a trick to get her to open the door? If she opened the shutter, she could see what was out there, but whatever was out there might see the shutter move and know she was looking.

There were more windows upstairs, if she—

Another howl knifed through her resolve—

Ahhwooooo-wwoooo-wwooo!

She stepped back.

"More are coming…they will be here soon…I am alone…trapped…I have nowhere else to go."

Something resonated deep in Casey's heart when the voice said it was alone, and her eyes fixed on the door with an abruptly fierce aspect not unlike her father's, miles away on a rooftop in Storm Town.

Father had said, "*Don't go outside.*"

It wouldn't be the first time she disobeyed his wishes. Though she never really meant or wanted to. In some way she didn't really understand, and couldn't explain, there were times she just knew that she had to.

And, Casey decided, this was one of them.

With fingers curled tight around the gun in her right hand and the comforting weight of the spare bullets in her pocket, Casey padded quietly to a position beside the door and laid her left hand on the bolt.

Ahhwooooo-wwoooo-wwooo!

Her back to the wall, Casey unlocked the door as quietly as she could—and whisked it open.

Nothing growled.

Nothing charged inside.

Casey took several breaths to slow her heart. Then, sliding down to peer around from near the floor like her father had taught her, she gasped at what she saw.

Sheriff Tanner was outgunned on the street five to four.

The quintet kept walking after the sheriff hailed them, and he let them go for half a dozen paces, increasing the distance between them and thereby improving the sight lines for Jonas and that deadly rifle of his. Wouldn't do having Jonas hit a deputy or the sheriff himself by mistake.

"That's far enough!" Tanner finally shouted. "You lot are under arrest. Surrender or be taken into custody by force."

The five stopped and turned around. One of them took a step forward. "What's the charge, sheriff? We just got into town and done no wrong."

"You lot are known Red Ridge Riders."

The man put his hands on his hips, and all three deputies quickly reached for their holsters.

The man smirked, then asked, "Since when is it a crime to have friends, then?"

"Since you and your friends rustled cattle over at Willow Pond."

"Heard 'bout that," the cowboy continued. "Nasty stuff. Rancher knocked senseless by masked men. Lost half his herd and half his teeth." At that two of the men beside him snickered. "Hands run off. No witnesses. And no way to prove these allegations, sheriff."

Tanner smirked right back at him. "Lost his teeth, you say? And how would you know that, unless you were there?"

The man's eyes widened for a moment, and those behind him tensed at the mistake their spokesman had made. Then the speaker regained his composure. "People talk, sheriff. 'Specially out on the trail. Can't right remember who told me the news. Gosh darn if it was the rustlers you're lookin' for! I might never forgive myself."

He's stalling, Jonas thought, *but for what?*

Then a flicker in the corner of his eye drew his attention back to the saloon. A pistol was creeping out over the swinging door, preparing to fire on the sheriff and his men from behind.

Jonas's lips tightened into a grim line.

"That is unfortunate," Tanner replied casually. "But no worm in the apple. As it turns out, you've been misinformed."

"How's that, sheriff?"

"I do have a witness," Tanner said with a smile. "The victim himself."

"The victim!" The man laughed. "How can he identify a masked man?"

Tanner nodded. "Masked men did rap him in the mouth with their guns, as you seem to know quite clearly. But that didn't stop him from getting a good long look at the man who let his mask down behind him—in the mirror."

"Mirror?" the man asked.

"That's right. And then he saw that man right here in the saloon tonight while he was easin' his pain with a whiskey. You." Sheriff Tanner pointed at the spokesman. "I'd say next time keep your mask on, but I figure you haven't got a next time coming."

Now it was the deputies who snickered, while up above Jonas held his sights on the hand holding the gun in the doorway. *Tough shot. The deputies wouldn't be laughing if they knew there was a gunman at their backs.*

Jonas could shout a warning, but reckoned that at least one of them was still likely to be shot in the ensuing confusion. It was up to him. A hard choice that required a cold answer.

A violent answer.

Just like in the war.

Jonas knew Tanner didn't like to go for the gun first—but shoot first, that was another matter entirely.

"That so, sheriff?" the rustler growled. "'Cause right now I like my odds a lot better—"

BAMM!

Jonas fired at the pistol-bearing hand.

The door splintered, and the gun-hand jerked back into the saloon.

Below Jonas the nature and whereabouts of the gunshot triggered a moment of confusion, then the street exploded with gunfire, and in the muzzle flashes that lit up the darkened lane, Jonas clearly saw the first man to go down.

Deputy Mills.

"Rotten thieves," Jonas snarled, reloading and drawing a new sight line. Two heartbeats later Liberty shouted into the night a second time and one of the rustlers landed on his back.

The combatants dashed off in different directions—some seeking cover, others trying to make moving targets of themselves.

Another cowboy fell to the ground. When he tried to rise and resume firing, Sheriff Tanner ran up close and shot him twice in the torso.

Their odds had gotten even quick, but before Tanner could take cover again, he was shot in the shoulder and corkscrewed down to one knee. The pivot miraculously saved his life—the next two rounds whistled over his head instead of lodging in his chest. Eyes wide he flopped to the dirt and rolled as fast as he could under the protection of the boardwalk.

Perhaps because he had shot the sheriff or perhaps because he was just closest, Hob and Jenkins opened fire simultaneously on Tanner's assailant, striking him multiple times. The man dropped his gun, bounced off a hitching post, and then fell face first into the dirt.

The fourth man pulled two pistols. After taking down Deputy Mills, he began to backpedal, firing erratically, sometimes at the sheriff and his men and sometimes at Jonas, during which he lodged a round in the A in JACK and the last L in WALL of the store sign. Perched over the W, Jonas didn't blink or duck. Liberty rang out a third time, and Storm Town's unique brand of rooftop justice was served yet again.

The street quieted.

The last Red Ridge Rider had taken cover behind a barrel, no doubt deciding whether to run, fight, or surrender. Tanner's orders were the same every time he deputized him, so Jonas knew it really didn't matter what the man did unless he threw down his weapons.

"Once the shooting starts, they all get pine boxes," the sheriff reminded his deputies during weapons check. "Unless they drop their guns and surrender, they all go down, even if they're running. If they don't go down, they come back with friends and we have to do this all over again. Understand?"

They did.

The war between North and South might have ended, but survival and prosperity in the West was a new battle every day. Some, like today, were more dangerous than others.

As Hob and Jenkins closed in on him, the rustler broke like a spooked mule.

As soon as he ran, it was obvious why—the man was fast on his feet. Both deputies opened fire with their Peacemakers but couldn't seem to hit their zigzagging target.

Jonas frowned. Graveyards in the West were full of men killed or ambushed from behind, just like the gunman in the saloon had planned to do to Storm Town's lawmen, but aside from the battlefield and despite Tanner's speech, the next time Jonas put a bullet in someone's back on purpose would be the first time.

Jonas raised his rifle, but the speeding man finally went down, relieving him of the grim duty.

Hob smiled and waved his hat at him, claiming the shot with pride. Knowing it wasn't time to celebrate just yet, Jonas called down, "Tanner! One more in the saloon. Didn't see his face. Send the others in, and I'll cover you all from here."

Despite his left sleeve being dark with wet blood, the sheriff remained determined to lead the way and strode purposefully into the Aces High with his deputies. Jonas grimaced at the pain he knew Tanner must be feeling and found yet another layer of respect for the brave man before him.

A short time later, they returned to the street empty-handed. The mysterious sixth man had escaped through the rear of the establishment during the gunfight.

Jonas exhaled. This one was over.

For now at least.

Though Jonas had survived years of battlefields, and even a hunt down into the Cave of Bones under Thunder Peak, he still felt a rush of relief after every gun battle. Shootouts were just so different from the war, where the fighting could last hours, days even. In the street matters were settled in swift, violent seconds.

But this time one had gotten away. When one man goes to jail or gets hung, a gang sometimes comes looking for misguided retribution. When five men get pine boxes, gangs usually get the message. So there was a good chance the Red Ridge Riders would leave the area. Maybe fifty-fifty, Jonas surmised. It all depended on their leader, especially if he was in one of the pine boxes.

Right then. Nothing else for it tonight—Jonas knew—*but to wait and hope for the best. Time now to pick up the pieces and bury the dead. Poor Mills. The sheriff is going to need a new deputy.*

Jonas sighed. He'd have to spend the night at the sheriff's office, though. Just in case. Still, with a little luck, he would make it back home, back to Casey, by morning. Maybe even before she woke. That was something.

Casey stood in the doorway trying to reconcile the bloody moonlit scene before her.

All that noise! It had been a battle between a wild stallion and a wolf!

Now both of them lay in the grass covered in blood. When Casey stepped outside the door, she could plainly see that the wolf's chest was pummeled and its face caved, as if struck by a giant hammer.

The horse lay on its side and startled Casey into a quick breath when it looked up at her.

The young colt was bleeding from numerous bites and claw marks about its body. Despite the carnage, Casey's eyes were drawn to the horse's mane and fixed there. The plume was glowing like silvery moonlight, or perhaps it was starlight.

The horse neighed softly, looking at her. Then its weary eyes seemed to focus on the gun in her hand and the great head dropped down heavily with a resigned snort.

Casey waited, watching the darkness with the pistol in her little hand, listening to the heavy breathing of the injured horse and glancing back every so often at its sparkling mane.

The voice in her head had disappeared. The only thing that made sense was that it belonged to the horse, but that was silly, wasn't it? Yet the voice had said it was injured…that it needed her help…and here was the horse, injured and needing her help. Why would it stop talking to her now that she had finally come out?

Judging from its injuries, Casey figured the horse must have fought off several wolves and the pack hadn't attacked again because she was standing there. Going back inside and closing the door would kill the horse as surely as the teeth and claws of the pack that was no doubt hoping she would do just that.

At that thought Casey's fingers tightened around the Navy's grip, and deciding she couldn't let those wolves kill this beautiful horse, she stepped outside.

Casey walked delicately around the steed, wondering, *Did you really kill this wolf?*

Then a howl rose up from the surrounding woods, reminding her that the fallen wolf's packmates remained near at hand. *Why? Flee or attack, what are they waiting for?* Then she answered her own question. *The rest of the pack to come.* At least, that's what the voice had said while she was still inside.

Casey knelt down and stroked the horse's glowing mane. "Were you really talking to me or did I just imagine that?" she asked him.

With a sharp jerk, the animal's head came up and around to peer directly into her eyes.

"Silver?" she gasped at the amount of intelligence she saw staring back at her. "I've seen blue before, even yellow once…but not silver."

After several long moments, the horse let out a long breath and lay back down.

"I knew you were out here, in trouble," she continued soothingly. "I want to help." Another howl rent the air, this one closer. "Okay. So, first thing is to get inside. That means you have to stand. Then I'll take you to the barn; it's not far, just over there." She pointed.

The horse turned its head to look.

"Yes, see?" Casey said, voice tinged with astonishment. "We must have a bond. Like some people have with their dogs, and horses too. I think I heard that somewhere. Like the Indians have with the land. Maybe that's how I knew you were out here in trouble."

The horse took another deep, rasping breath and struggled up on shaking legs, trembling like a newborn calf as the blood from several ragged wolf bites dripped over its flanks and ran down its legs.

"Easy," Casey said. "We can make it, and from inside I can protect you. I'm a very good shot."

With its glowing mane lighting the way, Casey led the horse toward the barn. The animal stepped slowly, whinnying softly each time its weight fell toward the left. Casey pulled the door wide, and just as the horse crossed inside, it shuddered violently.

Casey got an eerie sensation in her back and shoulders—raised her gun and spun about in one fluid motion.

Nothing.

The gun barrel tracked back and forth, but there was just silence and dark as far as her eyes could see.

As the seconds dragged on and nothing charged out of the night to attack her, Casey felt her breathing slow and a great wave of fear return. It was like the brave girl she had just been had disappeared and she was herself again. The gun began to wobble in her hand.

"First your heart, then your hands," she whispered, backing into the barn. After several steps she bumped into the horse, waiting and watching behind her.

"In! In!" she hissed urgently. The horse retreated with her, and then she closed the big door and bolted it as fast as she could.

"Get home soon, Dad," she said quietly. "Please. Come home soon."

3
NIGHTBLADE

Perched at the edge of the woods near the Tamm homestead, a simmering cloud pulsing with malevolent life and intelligence hovered close to the ground. Blacker than the darkness around it, the inky spectral energy sometimes ebbed and stretched up to fifteen feet across; other times it coalesced into a tight sphere only inches around. Yet no matter the shape and size in which the gentle woodland animals and birds found it, they gave the essence a wide berth because its aura was unwavering.

Pernicious, their instincts told them. Predator. Run!

Nightblade did not like to come to this place, the home of the abomination. He had almost died near here at the hands of the golden-haired elfwitch. The aril scout was long gone now, back through the portal, back home, but not before destroying his physical body, leaving Nightblade powerless, incorporeal, and stranded in this horrible land where the faerie blood and magic he needed to regain his strength was all but extinct.

The Nightblade was a unique and powerful creature. Chieftain of the great saber-toothed wolf nation known as the Cree and a being that could only be truly slain in its faerie homerealm of Leutia. So how the elfwitch and her accursed shell warrior construct had defeated and trapped his essence here was still a mystery to him.

In Leutia he was a mighty, magical beast of fang and claw, stalking prey from the Copper Cliffs of Collantis to the icy maw of the Volcano of Frost. Now he was but a ghostly prisoner, trapped in the awful human realm of Earther, clinging to existence as a living shadow that embraced the night. He could move but had to be careful, for in daylight he could be easily spotted by humans unless hugging the dark ground or nestled in tangled, leafy branches. Though they could not kill him, humans did have an abundance of silver, which caused Nightblade excruciating pain.

Still, robbed as he was of his frightening physical strength and magic, his mind remained powerful enough to influence the fanged folk and other denizens of Earther's animal kingdom, and so he had come to rule a vicious pack of wolves that he considered his subjects.

Mournfully, it was to him a pitiful kingdom that he reigned over, and Nightblade despaired. For true as it was that he could not be slain here, without faerie sustenance he would eventually lose his grip on even the spectral existence he maintained. When that happened Nightblade would simply cease to exist. But that would take a long, long time. The fact was that the elfwitch had cursed him with a fate worse than death, and the only solace Nightblade had while he haunted the area around the hidden portal through which he had originally come was that he was one day closer to that final release.

That is…until today.

Today—when the rune stones of the dormant portal that linked Earther and Leutia abruptly crackled with energy and flared to life.

Today—when the portal unexpectedly opened and geysered the aromas of magic and faerie blood.

Blood of the mane.

More importantly, a source of vital blood magic that could recharge his frein and restore his physical form!

Like embers cast from a bonfire, magical sparks sputtered and spewed from the portal when it came to life. Widening into a dark puddle, Nightblade swallowed and absorbed them as they fell, recharging his eldritch abilities and sharpening his sluggish mind.

Then unicorns began vaulting through the gateway, and for the first time since his physical destruction, the Cree Chieftain felt fully alert. His initial instinct was to summon the pack to attack his natural enemies. But more than just mighty, Nightblade was shrewdly clever, the ultimate foe of every animal, magical or otherwise, that lived around him, and so he checked his faerie-lust with tactics that satisfied his long-term goals, not his immediate desires.

Why a herd of the faerie mane had come to the human realm was inconsequential to him. The only way home for them, and him, was back through the portal. This was denied Nightblade in his current condition; only flesh and blood could pass through the gate. Incorporeal beings who tried to cross through inevitably set off chain reactions that forced it to close.

But perhaps, he realized suddenly, that was something he could now use to his advantage.

Though Nightblade knew his best course was to wait, curiosity got the better of him, and so he followed and watched from afar as the mane-folk searched out rare trees of white, splintering bark scattered deep in the woods around the foot of the mountain. Even from a distance, Nightblade could sense the latent frein energy growing and stored in those wintry-colored limbs and their sky-colored fruit, but they were useless, even dangerous, to him.

Nightblade was the spawn of shadow and a carnivore; he could not gain sustenance from magical fruit, especially if it was saturated with golden frein.

The unicorns harvested the trees by placing their head spikes against them. The magic of their horns imbued the trees with life and vigor that shook them until they splintered and shrugged away their older branches in favor of fresh, clean bark and perky sprouts that would one day grow into strong new limbs. The unicorns pierced the fruit among the trimmings with their horns, causing them to glow, and then absorbed the twinkling light straight into their sparkling head spikes until the fruit shriveled away into nothing.

Nightblade was unsure of the purpose of this ritual—perhaps the unicorns empowered themselves through organic magic the same way the Cree did through blood magic. Whatever the purpose truly was, Nightblade surmised that he might be the very first of the Cree to witness such a harvesting; information that could prove valuable someday if he ever returned home.

When they finished, the herd dashed off with frightening speed to the next tree, the mighty tramp of their hooves shaking everything around them like thunder.

The Cree Chieftain wasn't sure he could keep pace with them even in the true wolfen form that had been denied him. But he didn't have to. He knew where they must eventually go to get back home.

The portal. And so he got their first, blending into the smudges and growth hugging the stones around the magical archway until the herd returned.

It would be painful, but if he struck the gate and absorbed what he could before it closed, Nightblade would gain even more magical power. If he could strike the gate at just the right moment, he could also force it to disconnect and trap the last of the herd.

Then he would have to work quickly.

First to summon his earthly wolf pack to fell the steed as fast as possible;

once the unicorn was down, Nightblade could siphon its frein directly from its wounds. Though many forms of magic, including that of the portal, could be harvested to replenish his powers, only with faerie blood could his physical body be permanently restored.

Naturally Nightblade knew he wouldn't have time to consume the entire juvenile, nor did he really need too. Just enough to attain the physical form he needed to make his own frein self-sustaining. He'd never been this weak before, so whether that meant one bite or ten, he did not know.

What he did know was that starving as he was, he would be quick to consume all he required.

Nightblade yearned to get home. But there was also the mission his hidden aril ally expected him to complete.

The Cree Chieftain simply could not bear the thought of his battle with the elfwitch and his exile in the human realm being all for nothing. There was too much at stake. Success was paramount.

He would finish what he had set out to do, and with the aril scout gone, there would be no one to stop him.

Then, at long last, it would be time for the aril to keep their promises and return to the Cree what was rightfully theirs.

In time, of course, he would find the blond witch that had exiled him here. And if she yet lived, Nightblade would first assure her that his return meant her offspring was dead, impaled on his saber-tooth fangs. Then he would paint his teeth with her soft flesh and send the witch to join her abomination in the next life.

Initially the plan went better than he ever could have hoped.

Initially. The herd returned at dusk, and watching carefully as the mane-folk began passing through the gate one at a time, he saw the last in line was a juvenile, but even so, the grace and power with which it already moved foretold it would be an formidable steed in the future.

Timing his strike to the instant, Nightblade rose into the portal when the juvenile was in mid gallop. The steed cried out in alarm at the sudden appearance of the inky cloud filling the gateway before him but bravely leaped into the closing eldritch arch anyway.

When the juvenile struck, the innate magic of both faerie creatures interacted with the magic of the gate. The shadow frein of the Cree and the golden frein of the unicorn repelled each other naturally, hurling them away from the portal in opposite directions. But only after the rune magic of the gate smote them to the core with an excruciating eldritch blast.

The juvenile neighed in pain, a mournful, soul-shattering sound that Nightblade barely heard over the searing pain flaring in his spiritual synapses.

Both of them collapsed, the horse with a log-heavy thud, Nightblade dispersing to the limits of his mind.

The sheer misery of trying to pull his spectral being back together forced him to lose consciousness for a time. When he finally awoke, Nightblade thought for sure it was to failure, that the juvenile had already been recovered by its herd.

But no! The juvenile still lay where it had fallen, still unconscious.

Confusion set in. Why did the unicorns not return? It was unlike the manefolk to leave a survivor behind in battle, let alone abandoned among the Earthers. Perhaps striking the gate together had not only forced it to close but also damaged it in some way. Whatever the cause, Nightblade surmised that aril gatekeepers were working hard to get it open again. How long the opportunity to restore himself would last was unknown, but he was determined to seize the moment before it was lost.

Reaching out with his mind, Nightblade summoned the pack to come and slay the juvenile, but the steed shuddered awake and rose unsteadily to its feet at their approaching howls.

As the moon rose higher and the clouds cleared, its flowing mane and tail began to glow with silvery starlight, a vision that would have driven Nightblade mad with hunger in his physical form.

Coming fully alert, the creature paced, snorting and stamping before stopping suddenly, as if sensing something. In the next instant, the steed bolted away into the wood and the hunt was on.

Watching it thunder off made Nightblade roil with pleasure. Distance would make the juvenile harder for any would-be rescuers to find, and a true hunt would be fun. After all, there was nowhere for it to go.

Or so Nightblade thought.

Sending out a silent call for the pack to track the steed, the Cree billowed slowly after it through the woods.

Then Nightblade realized where the juvenile was going and pulsed in frustration. If only he could move faster! Do something tangible. Anything! But no; the witch had seen to that.

He willed the others to slow the juvenile down until he could get there to witness the kill, but these instructions were misinterpreted and some of the wolves attacked.

One of them paid dearly with injuries and death at the formidable hoof of the juvenile. Two others escaped, one with grievous wounds. That animal limped away in the night toward the mountain, most likely to perish in peaceful solitude instead of having the pack fall on it.

The rest waited, assembling in greater strength, and Nightblade knew it was only a matter of time before they attacked again if he was not on hand to keep them in check.

It was then, upon arriving at the human dwelling, that he saw the girl take the horse toward the barn. Even from a distance he could sense the powerful protection magic still in place around each structure, so strong that even if he were at full power, Nightblade would be unable to enter for very long, if at all. In this the aril witch continued to surprise him. How had she attained such mastery?

Nightblade paused to consider his next move, but the evening valley breeze shifted slightly and broke his concentration almost immediately. For laced into the new current the wolf lord sensed an aura that he had missed for so, so long.

Blood.

A burst of excitement rippled over and through Nightblade's shadow.

Mane-folk blood!

There by the human dwelling! The juvenile must have fallen!

To ensure he was not interrupted, Nightblade acted swiftly, urging the pack to swarm and circle the barn, growling and scratching at every corner.

Meanwhile the shadow Cree glided low to the ground and descended first on the largest blood stain, then quickly moved on to the next. However slightly, the Cree Chieftain felt his frein reserve building with each morsel.

Upon finishing he flowed back to the wood. No longer just an insubstantial spectral shade, he now had the power to coalesce briefly into his saber-toothed, wolfen form. A feat through which he would be better able to lead and dominate the pack. Perhaps even summon more fangs to his side, increasing the pack's numbers and strength.

Sadly, he was still a long way from being able to go home, but if he could hold his likeness long enough, he might perform a jevaling—such was the instant power of blood magic.

For the first time since his physical destruction, Nightblade could howl and be heard, but this he did not do. His frein was limited and would not be self-sustaining until he completely regained his physical form. Therefore, it was imperative he used the power he had attained wisely.

Nightblade settled down, retreating to where he could watch the barn and the house. As much as he wanted to attack, he remembered well the circumstances under which the aril spell weaver had defeated him. And though the scout had long since departed, there was no doubt the shell warrior she had made to aid her in battle and left behind to watch over her witchling patrolled somewhere close by. Long he had watched that one. The reptilian was a formidable obstacle to him regaining his full power, but once he did, the shell warrior would be no match for the Cree Chieftain.

Too he must consider that the witch may have left weapons for the humans that could deplete his frein. Plus, there was still the possibility of rescue coming for the juvenile, a rescue that may already be on its way.

With so many variables in motion, the Cree knew that what it needed most now was a plan.

A plan to bleed the juvenile.

A plan that included destroying the offspring and returning home to his kindred victorious.

Nightblade growled, and the remaining wolves around him shrank away, leaving the Cree to ponder and plan. For beyond even the power of his jaws, his frightening speed, and even his unique ability to shadow leap was the Cree Chieftain's cunning. So it was that Nightblade set his mind to work without worry. He knew ideas and the moves to execute them would come, just as they always did.

And then, one way or another, the juvenile's blood would be his.

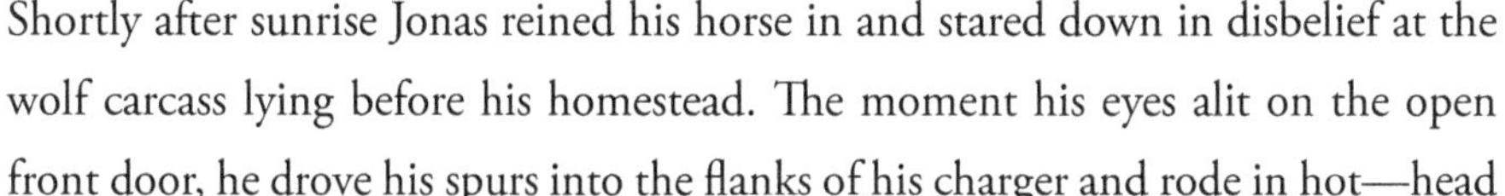

Shortly after sunrise Jonas reined his horse in and stared down in disbelief at the wolf carcass lying before his homestead. The moment his eyes alit on the open front door, he drove his spurs into the flanks of his charger and rode in hot—head low against the horse's neck and pistol drawn.

Heart thudding in his chest—not from what might be about to happen but rather what might have already transpired—Jonas pulled the horse up sharp and tight beyond view of the door and quickly dismounted.

Both guns drawn and cocked, he took a position just to the side of the door and whistled like a spring bird. When no reply came from within, he feared the worst, took a steadying breath, and followed the barrels of his 1873 Colt .45s inside.

Faced with no ambush and no threat within the house, his brow furrowed in confusion.

"Casey!" he finally called out. "Casey! Where are you?"

Back at the door, it took only a cursory examination to see it had not been broken in. The place was in perfect order. *Alice's Adventures in Wonderland* lie unattended on the couch.

"Casey!" Jonas called out again, sweat breaking off his forehead.

He checked everywhere, then stepped back out on the porch and eyed the dirt.

Tracks. Lots of them. Mostly wolves. Wolves like he hadn't seen since…

One horse too.

The wolf's face and ribs had been kicked in.

A powerful horse.

Had one of the animals Casey saw yesterday followed her here?

Jonas looked more closely at the prints and picked out a set that could only be Casey's leading off to the barn.

Heart racing anew, he holstered one gun and dashed to the barn. As he drew near, one of the doors opened just a little and Jonas threw himself to the dirt, rolled, and came up in a combat stance, ready for the worst.

A walnut-tressed head poked out between the doors.

"Casey!" Jonas shouted with relief and rose quickly to his feet. "Casey!"

The girl looked at him with wide eyes and then slipped out and rushed toward him. “Daddy!” she cried back, and when they took each other up in arms, both of them had tears in their eyes.

“Daddy!” She sobbed. “I’m sorry I opened the door, but I had to.”

“It’s okay Nightingale,” he said, hugging her tight. “Everything is okay. Is it okay?” he asked suddenly, pulling back to look at her. She nodded. “Okay good.” He pulled her in close again and ran his free hand up and down her back in long soothing sweeps. “I’m here now.”

After a time Casey regained her composure, and before Jonas could ask her anything, she told him. “You have to come into the barn. Come and see him.”

Jonas tilted his head while his right hand dipped back to his holster. “See who?”

“He doesn’t have a name yet,” Casey said. “I suppose…can I name him? Please, Daddy! You always say fair is fair. I saved him; I should get to name him.”

“Saved who?” Jonas wondered aloud as he entered the barn. Then he just stopped and stared, gripping Casey’s hand so tightly that she catapulted back toward him when she reached the end of his arm’s length.

The horse, if indeed that was all it was, was magnificent, its coat a glossy black, its mane and tail a striking, feathery white, like ocean foam.

Jonas and the horse made eye contact, and in that instant, he knew for certain that this was no ordinary animal and quite possibly from the other side.

From her side.

“Casey, is this one of the horses you saw yesterday?”

Casey looked at the steed with open delight. “I’m not sure. There were so many. It could be, but he doesn’t have a horn.”

“Right,” Jonas said, feeling as though the horse was studying him as much as he was it.

“I helped him as best I could,” Casey said, walking over slowly to the horse and petting his neck. "The cuts look awful ragged, but none of them are very deep."

Jonas looked over the horse's wounds and said, "You did good, real good cleaning and dressing his wounds."

Then he nodded, getting an idea, and to the steed he said, "You are safe here. Wait and rest, and we'll fetch something that should help those bites heal faster."

Jonas and the horse held each other's gaze for a moment, and then the homesteader turned away.

"Come with me, Casey," he said, taking her hand and leading her out of the barn. "This...new friend of yours might need something special to help him heal."

"Something special?"

"Yes," Jonas answered. "Ice apples from the pearlwood."

"What apples?" Casey asked, but she quickly forgot her question when her father left the barn doors open. "Wait!" she called out. "The doors! What if he runs off?"

"That's up to him."

Casey looked at her father like he had been kicked in the head.

When he saw the look on her face, he laughed. "Don't worry. I think he'll stay."

"He will?"

Jonas nodded. "Like I said, he's more than just a horse."

"But what does that mean?" Casey gave her father a discerning look. "You promised we'd continue talking when you got back."

Jonas nodded again. "I know. And we will. But right now we have this to take care of."

Casey stamped her foot and folded her arms, but before she could speak, her father said, "You obviously helped this horse last night, maybe even saved his life. Do you really want to risk one of his wounds getting infected and having to put him down after all that, just because you can't wait a few more hours to talk?"

Casey looked at the barn, heaved a deep sigh, and turned back to her father. "No."

"Good." Jonas smiled. "Now, into the house, get your leathers. And Casey…" Jonas waited until they made eye contact. "Be sure to bring your mother's throwing knives."

Casey looked down for a moment, then nodded and ran off.

Sparing it the same consideration she would any other woodland obstacle, Casey blissfully vaulted over the dead wolf and closed the door behind her.

While Casey was in the house preparing for their journey, Jonas retrieved a rope from the barn to hang and drain the wolf carcass for skinning. No sense wasting good fur.

Yesterday, when Casey said she had seen magical horses, he had focused on it as a reason to tell her the truth. Fretting over that, he failed to consider what it could mean for him. Having just seen one of the horses for himself, it began to sink in.

With a long sigh, he tied off the final knots, pondering how long he had waited for a sign like this. *Too long*, he thought, finishing his grisly task. Despair had won that battle long ago. So long ago Jonas knew he too could wait a little bit longer for answers, especially now that there was a ray of light on the horizon. What it all meant he didn't know, but he meant to find out.

Casey came out of the house with her gun belt on, and Jonas frowned. "I told you to bring the knives."

"I brought the knives." Casey spread her arms to better show him the shoulder sash lined with throwing blades and the long silver knife sheathed at her left hip.

Jonas pursed his lips.

"No matter how good I am, I can only throw the knives so far, Dad…"

"True enough." Jonas reluctantly agreed. "All right, then. But that pistol stays skinned until I say otherwise."

"Yes, Dad," Casey answered, but in her heart she was sure that after this adventure, after she proved herself a good shootist like him, he would learn to trust her more often and that would be the end of the smothering, silly knives.

She just didn't see the use. Knives were for circus performers, not deputies, sheriffs, and marshals. Because that's what Casey intended to be. The first woman marshal.

Maybe after this adventure, she could tell her father about her aim to help those in search of justice find it, just like he did when the sheriff needed him.

The kind of justice her parents never got.

After.

What she did not realize—and nor did her father—was that in her haste Casey had packed only three of her mother's silver knives; the remaining seven were her practice steel.

Lurking in the murky morning shadow cast by a nearby boulder, a pair of sinister red eyes watched the humans go.

Nightblade had heard all.

If the hoof juvenile required magical sustenance to help it heal, the humans must be going to one of the trees the unicorns harvested. Probably the nearest. In his physical form, getting there first would be simple. Unfortunately, Nightblade could sense the silver the pair had armed themselves with and did not wish to waste any of his newly acquired frein in a confrontation that would accomplish little, if anything.

The wolf pack he reigned over, would also be of little use against the humans and their firesticks. His real pack, dwelling back home on the Copper Cliffs, would obey him immediately and destroy the humans easily. Certainly a few would perish in the attack. The humans had so much silver here, unfathomable amounts, and this made them quite dangerous. But the Cree were some two feet larger at the shoulder than typical wolves, and the most powerful could even leap through shadow like Nightblade himself. Swiftly surrounded and overwhelmed by numbers, the humans would be annihilated. But these lesser cousins of Earther, they could not move in shadow and were injured easily by lesser weapons such as wood and iron. They also feared fire and cowered easily when their brothers fell. When a Cree saw its brother or sister fall in battle, it doubled its efforts to take down the prey.

Nightblade breathed deep, drawing himself back to the moment and the problem at hand.

Somehow, the juvenile needed to be lured out of it place of protection. Outside where it could be damaged and Nightblade could feed and grow stronger, but in such a way that the Cree would not reveal himself. For now, and until his powers could be further restored, being hidden was his greatest asset.

First things first.

The shell guardian that the elfwitch had left behind. The one who had helped her defeat him. It would show itself soon and must be dealt with.

But how?

Naturally, beings that preferred the light were more susceptible to manipulation and subterfuge, but how best to employ that against a lonely shell guardian?

Then his gaze alit on a colorful lizard darting through the brush, and it gave him an idea. An idea that swiftly inspired plans within plans, for the mind of the Cree Chieftain was perfectly suited to complex machinations.

For the plan to work, Nightblade would need soldiers. Soldiers of old. Thankfully, the frein-laden blood of the juvenile he had found on the ground had imbued him with just enough power to perform the jevaling magic required.

Indeed, a *making* would prove too mysterious and tempting for his enemies to ignore. Such was their way.

Such was their weakness.

And just like that, the pieces clicked into place. A moment ago Nightblade only had a goal; now he possessed the vision to see it through.

Reaching out with his mind, Nightblade detected a nest of the leaping, darting lizards full of eggs, glided over, and settled upon it.

The jevaling spell would deplete nearly all the frein he had gained from both the gate's rune energy and the blood magic gleaned from the unicorn, reducing him once again to just his spectral form. In truth, Nightblade hated the idea of giving up access to his physical body so soon after reclaiming it, but the sacrifice was necessary; in the vision there was everything to gain and nothing to lose.

A lesser creature might try to find another way, but not Nightblade; keen was the discipline of the Cree Chieftain once his goal was fixed.

Taking solace in the fact that throughout history the scaled folk had proven themselves the best of pawns, Nightblade wove his dark energy into a spell of *making*. Using it to infuse the eggs with magical malice and power, he hatched an entirely new creature, a ferocious, cold-blooded engine of tooth and claw that would inspire its own host of Thunder Peak nightmares.

4

TALIKO

Jonas and Casey picked their way south through the canopied woods while all around them birds chirped and small animals scurried out of their path. Up above the morning sun streamed down at sharp angles through tall pines, aspens, and cottonwoods.

Pausing a moment to take it all in, Jonas took a deep breath.

He loved the valley.

As a Texan, Jonas thought he'd never see so many trees again after the war and was surprised by how much he began to miss them. After making the decision to leave, he'd thought often as the dry, sunbaked miles passed under his wagon that perhaps he'd made a mistake. That instead of moving west through Texas and into Mexico and then north into the Arizona Territory, he should have gone east, where he stood a better chance of finding some vibrant woods again.

He still wasn't sure what had pressed him to enter the dark defile lurking in the shadow of the mountain he now knew as Thunder Peak. But the moment the rugged trail opened into a secluded, lush canyon full of trees, he knew he was home.

Later Jonas learned that he had wandered into Itza Chu Canyon via "The Back Door." Discovering secluded Storm Town hidden within, cloaked in all its legends and populated by fugitive ruffians in search of a fresh start, only made it better.

Jonas glanced back at Casey. Interrupted only by bird song, they'd traveled in silence for nearly thirty minutes, which he thought quite remarkable considering the circumstances. Then again, he had to admit, in that way Casey could be very thoughtful and introspective, like her mother.

Jonas wiped his brow with a kerchief tied around his neck. Deciding it might be best to casually break the silence, he waited until they set off again before asking, "What happened? Last night, with the wolf?"

Casey took a deep, shuddering breath. "It was awful, Dad. There was all this scary howling, getting closer and closer. Then something came up to the door. First I thought it was a bear because it…" Casey trailed off.

Jonas looked at Casey and saw her wrestling with the words. "It's okay," he said. "I know you opened the door after I told you not to. I tell you that to be safe from strangers who might happen upon our property. But sometimes, if the reasons are well enough, you have to take a risk. You made a good decision. I'm not mad at you. Quite the opposite. I'm right proud of the way you handled yourself, especially knowing how you feel about wolves."

Casey exhaled, obviously relieved. "So, taking risks is okay for good reasons, like when you get deputized?"

Jonas looked ahead through the woods, then nodded slowly. "Yes. Rather like that."

Casey nodded, wiped her forehead with her sleeve, and peered up through the branches at the August sun climbing slowly into the sky. It was already another hot day in the Arizona Territory.

They walked a little farther, picking up and following a regular game trail that crept up toward Thunder Peak. Then she continued, "I could hear fighting outside. It sounded terrible. I thought…I was worried about Cross and Cotton in the barn at first but…The growling and whinnying…It was right outside…"

Casey took a deep breath. She simply could not force herself to say, *The horse was talking to me in my head and was asking for my help, so I knew I had to open the door.*

He will understand, she told herself. *He's seen the horse in the barn, and he's going to believe me. He believed me when I said I saw horses with horns, and in the barn, he even talked to the horse like he was really listening, so why am I worried he won't believe me?*

Casey silently ridiculed herself. *Because he always talks to the horses and doesn't expect them to talk back, you cornstalk!*

The silence dragged on again until her father sighed and said, "So you thought maybe, in my haste, I hadn't locked up the barn. A wolf came sniffing around, spooking Cross or Cotton out of their stall and then got attacked. So you grabbed your iron to try and help him. Is that the right of it?"

"Well, it was all happening so fast," Casey answered, relieved at not having to explain in greater detail.

"It always does," Jonas said distantly. "Remember that feeling."

Casey looked at her father. "Is that how it is for you? When you help the sheriff?"

"Yes," he answered without looking at her.

Casey nodded again and took a long glance at him. He had taken off those dreadful spurs but was still wearing the rest of his deputy clothes and both of his guns. "I'm glad you only help him sometimes and not all the time."

Maybe being a marshal isn't such a good idea after all, she thought. *It's easy being brave around my dad, but last night, when I was alone, I was really scared and—*

Jonas halted suddenly and raised his hand in a fist, signaling her to stop and remain quiet.

Point Lookout had come into view, and after taking a long moment to scan the woods around them, her father pulled out his harmonica. The notes he forced from it were trill and startling, completely unlike anything Casey had ever heard him play before. When he finished he gestured for her to follow him through the fragrant regiment of dragon eye daisies surrounding the site and sit with him at the base of the looming, jagged wall.

They snacked quietly on jerky and apples under the stained-glass window while the sun climbed nearly into the noon sky. Sensing after a time that her father was alertly watching the creek—for what, she didn't know—Casey finally whispered into the quiet, "What are we waiting for, Dad?"

Jonas hesitated, then said, "To see if anything comes before we cross."

Casey looked at the woods with fresh eyes for a moment, then turned back to her father. But before she could pose another question, he said, "Right then, I guess it's just us. Let's go."

Just us? Casey pondered. *Who else would it be?*

Her father stood, and so did she, adjusting first her gun belt, then the leather knife sash. The rig hung crosswise from her right shoulder to her left hip, where her long knife was belted. It held four throwing knives down the front, one at the top of the back strap where she could reach it over her shoulder, and three more slung down her back. Casey felt the whole thing was cumbersome and said, "Looks spooky over there. Glad I've got my Navy with me to rely on 'stead of just a bunch of circus knives."

Silently she added, *I have to stay sharp and get anything that comes at us before he does. Once he sees that, he's sure to let me ditch this fool butcher's tack for good. He'll have to.*

Jonas stopped, turned, and gently lifted her angular chin so he could look his daughter in the eye.

"The only one you have to blame for your lack of confidence in your throwing arm is yourself. I can't force you to practice when I'm not home. Guns are not for children. I've told you that many, many times. Most upright towns won't even let you wear them around anymore, and that's the way of things down the road I 'spect. Least I hope so."

"Well, we ain't in town, are we?" Casey pointed out, her tone thick with defiance.

"No." Her father's voice took on an edge. "We are most definitely *not* in town. And we are about to cross into a territory where time was your silver blades would keep more dangers at bay than the lead in our bullets."

Time was? Casey wondered while her father took a deep breath.

"Now," Jonas continued, "I'm sorry. Sorry because there are a lot of things you need to know that I haven't told you yet, like why your knives are special. Like why I made you practice with them and put down animals we needed for meat and tack and fur while you were younger than most. How there have been things a lot more dangerous than wolves around here. But there are reasons. And while we're out here, you need to trust me and do exactly as I say."

"I trust you, Dad," Casey said.

"Good," Jonas smiled. "Now hopefully it don't come to it, but if it does, promise me you will be very dangerous to whatever opposes us."

Her father always said things like "very dangerous" and "threatening" instead of "shoot it" or "kill it." Casey wasn't really sure why, just as she wasn't sure why it sometimes bothered her and sometimes didn't.

What had bothered her from her toes to her scalp was the time Nash had made fun of her dad over it. Casey didn't warn Nash that day; she just tackled him and throttled him in the face. That hadn't lasted, though. Back then Nash was stronger and flipped her over easily. She could still see him straddling her, his lip bleeding. He didn't hit her back, just looked at her for a long moment, then got up and left. They hadn't spoken for a long while after that, nor did she tell her father that she was mad at him too for his fool expressions that made folks laugh behind his back. Oddly enough, the worst of the bunch were the so-called upright folk of Storm Town, not that there were very many.

Nash eventually apologized. And when Casey admitted that she wished her father didn't say the things he sometimes said, Nash surprised her by defending him: "Straight truth is, no one who wears a gun or stumbles out of the Aces High or even Sticky Jacks ever disrespects your father." Then he added how not that long ago he'd even seen some tough-looking ranch hands cross the street when they saw Jonas coming along. "I could tell they recognized him. More, they was afraid of him. That's when I knew it was time to apologize, so here I am."

Nash's apology had been very important to her. The row had happened after school several years ago but was still something she thought about on and off. Whenever she did, the outcome, as well as the uncanny fact that Nash could no longer flip her over or hold her down if she didn't want him to, made her smile. That said, and rather like the day Nash had carried her, she still didn't quite understand why either of those thoughts made her heart skip the way they did.

Casey sighed. Some days it felt like nothing in her life made any sense. And today was definitely one of those days. To her father she said, "I will."

"Good," he smiled tightly. "First your heart."

"Then your hands," Casey answered.

A startling gleam she had never seen before filled her father's eyes. Then he nodded, stroked her head once, and hugged her. "Okay, let's move."

Jonas led the way across the brook, and Casey marveled that his feet seemed to know the best way not to get wet, like he'd crossed it many times before.

Yet another question to add to the many she already had.

Casey glanced back at Point Lookout before it disappeared behind the trees, and her right hand instinctively went to the center scabbard across her chest when she saw a low branch move sharply. *Something darting away, a rabbit perhaps, maybe even an otter here by the water.* Her father's speech had made her jumpy, and she realized that her heart was racing. Turning away to catch up, she steadied her breathing for whatever lay ahead—as her father seemed certain there must be.

The way was clogged with bramble and thick brush, and it was another long, arduous hour until they espied a majestic, forty-foot-tall white bark tree with juicy-looking sky-blue fruit hanging in its branches.

Her father crouched down and together they paused to regard it for several long minutes.

"So that's it?" Casey finally whispered.

"That's it," Jonas answered. "Pearlwood. Not many of them around."

"The tree," Casey said with the muted urgency of a mouse dashing off under a bed of leaves. "Its bark sparkles in the sunlight just like your harmonica!"

"It should," her father said without looking. "This is where I got the timber for it."

Casey frowned. Looking around again she tried to see what her father was seeing and made an important observation, or at least she thought it was important: "It's quieter here—than on the other side of the river."

"Yes," he said in a pleased tone, eyes still darting around. "Yes, it is. And the way seems suddenly darker somehow, like we're walking into an ambush."

The moment after her father said it, Casey drew a knife from her sash. By mere chance she glanced at it and saw the grisly blue face hurtling down on her from above.

Casey rolled with a shout, thrusting the knife high, and the scaly creature impaled itself with a screech and crumpled on top of her. A second later it flared brightly into blue dust.

"Cave demon!" Jonas shouted, getting to his feet and waving the noisome vapors away with both hands.

When the smoke cleared, Jonas scanned the woods.

"We're surrounded," he hissed, lifting Casey to her feet.

Looking around, Casey saw reptilian faces appearing and disappearing in the brush and peeking around trees. Then, realizing that they had been discovered, the horde began to creep closer, teeth clacking, claws flexing.

Casey sucked in a fearful breath and began to mumble. "I've seen lizards that look like this. Red backs with yellow stripes. Blue faces and claws. Much smaller. In the woods."

No sooner had she heard the raspy whisper of metal on leather than the guns leaped from her father's hips and into his hands.

Jonas fired three quick shots, and the two nearest creatures collapsed.

The horde paused.

"Go!" her father ordered. "Get to the pearlwood!"

Casey bolted off while Jonas followed with slow, measured steps, guns tracking left and right like cobras, eyes riveted on the snarling, hissing lizardmen emerging from the dense woods.

Step for step the muscular creatures stalked them toward the white tree. Most of them walking upright, a little taller than a hitching post, some of them crawling, and a few carrying crude sharpened sticks like spears. They all glared at the humans, and in those serpentine eyes Casey saw hunger.

"Climb," Jonas hissed when he sensed the tree hovering over him, and Casey scampered up into the branches as easily as a squirrel.

With a deep, steadying breath, Jonas eyed the encroaching monsters until he felt the ivory tree trunk against his back.

Then, waiting until a handful crossed into the shade of the upper branches, he emptied his guns on them.

The scathing bullets tore into the pack with unrelenting fury, setting the entire lot scattering for safety. Praying this would give him time enough, Jonas holstered his weapons and began climbing up after his daughter as quickly as he could.

The barrage of bullets did set off a momentary panic among the lizardmen. However, realizing they had little to fear from lead in their magically evolved state, the snarling pack quickly found its courage and surged forward to attack their escaping prey.

Jonas was halfway up the tree and nearly out of reach when one of them propelled itself up with its powerful hind legs and grabbed his boot. The added weight made him lose his grip, and in the next moment, he was sliding back down.

Inch by excruciating inch, the bark scraped the skin from his grasping hands until finally he seized a passing branch and halted their descent.

No sooner had they stopped than Jonas felt a clamp on his knee and looked down—the scaly beast was trying to gnaw off his leg right through his buckskin pants.

Jonas swept his leg back and forth, gaining momentum, and then slammed the creature hard against the tree. The result was unexpected, but quite welcome, as the innate frein of the mysterious pearlwood, reacting instantly to the dark magic wound into the creature's body by Nightblade, sent sparkling silver shards into its scaly skin wherever they touched.

The beast yowled and fell away.

Jonas exhaled in relief, then looked up and even managed to get a hand on the next branch before catching a new motion in his eye: another demon had scampered up into the adjacent pine tree.

They made eye contact, and Jonas knew instantly that he'd discovered the threat too late to do anything about it. Claws extended, jaws agape, the creature was already in the air.

Jonas looked away, bracing himself for the bloodthirsty assault.

Thwip!

The deadly murmur of flying metal sliced the air.

Thuck!

Jonas swung his eyes back to find Casey had struck the creature deep in the mouth with a well-aimed throw!

Gurgling and choking, the creature reflexively snapped its jaws shut before crashing into Jonas. Disoriented by the pain, it neither scratched nor bit him before sliding away.

Regaining its senses in free fall, the lizardman instinctively slashed at the tree in an effort to save itself—and was promptly rewarded with sizzling bolts that sprang from the trunk and lanced into its hands and feet.

Suspended by the energy, the creature writhed in mid-air for a long moment. Then, with a loud crackling snap, the current repelled the reptile like a powerful magnet.

"Haah!" Jonas whooped, as the careening lizardman hit the ground with a bone-jarring smash.

Gasping but alive, the thing rolled over and began to rise. Hands smoking still, it wobbled unsteadily to its charred feet, then abruptly doubled over, retching and hacking until it regurgitated Casey's knife. Burns gently crackling and hissing, it then limped away on what appeared to be a broken leg.

Having seen all, Jonas grit his teeth and climbed higher into the branches, closer to Casey. Thirty feet up now, on the branch just below hers, he stopped to reload his guns from a black leather pouch instead of the rounds in his gun belt.

One of the monsters, seemingly more malevolent and intelligent than the rest, crouched down and watched them. When Jonas looked up to say something to Casey, the reptile struck.

Moving with great speed and dexterity, the creature dashed forward and hurled a wooden javelin. The missile was about a third of the length of a pool cue and buried itself in Jonas's thigh.

"Urrggh," Jonas grunted.

"Infernal demon!" he shouted, firing a quick shot at the scampering creature.

The scaly beast fell to all fours just in time, much to the misfortune of the member of the pack standing just beyond.

The reptile, hiss-laughing and celebrating its comrade's throw just a moment ago, was struck in the shoulder. Almost immediately the wound began to belch green smoke and flare like a firework. The flames spread quickly, consuming the stunned lizardman from snout to talon in seconds and leaving behind little more than a pile of sky-colored ash.

Jonas yanked the crude weapon out of his leg, broke it in two, and dropped the pieces.

Having set the example, the alpha lizard instructed the others to start gathering sticks and sharpening them with their jagged teeth.

Jonas counted nearly twenty-five lizardmen, but they moved in and out of the brush so fast he had no idea how accurate his headcount was.

"I don't understand. I hit that thing right in the throat; it should be dead." Casey shook her head. "Shot it. Like you did. That's what I should have done. But you were too close. Too risky. I did the right thing. Next time I'll—"

"Take one down now," her father said.

"What? Really? Just like that?"

"Just like that. Do it."

Casey took out her Navy .38 and pointed it at the lizardmen on the edge of the clearing. Aiming carefully, she took a deep, steadying breath, then another, before lowering her arm.

"Not as easy as it looks," her father said.

"No," Casey agreed. "I know they mean to attack us, but it's different when they're not. A lot different, I guess."

"I know," her father said softly. "Hearing you say that makes me glad. It's not supposed to be easy. But sometimes it's necessary, and right now it's necessary. So you can understand before it's too late."

"Understand what?"

"No more talk. Take one down. Now."

Casey nodded. Raised her pistol and after what seemed like a very long time, fired a shot. An instant later one of the lizards fell back like it had been yanked by a rope.

"There…" Casey began, her voice low. "I did—"

A woeful groan that turned into a bitter snarl cut Casey off, and she looked back to see the lizardman slowly picking itself up, rubbing its chest where its life should have been draining from a large hole. Shaking its fist, the monster glared and screeched at her.

Casey recoiled, suddenly fearful that the weapon that gave people dominance over the entire animal kingdom, and often enough one another, was useless. "What? How?"

"Did you see the ones I hit before I reloaded turn into dust? No. They were just stunned, and now they're back in the fight too."

"I don't understand," Casey said, still shaking her head.

"Only silver can hurt them," her father explained. "That's how you killed the first one. Your mother's knives are made of silver. But the second one didn't die, so you must have mixed some of your practice steel with your silver blades. Question right now is, how many silver knives did you bring?"

Casey sucked in a breath and checked herself in a panic. "Three! Only three! What are we going to do?"

Jonas turned away from the creatures and looked his daughter in the eye. "First your heart, then your hands."

Casey nodded rapidly, taking breaths in through her nose and exhaling out through the mouth in an effort to regain control of her breathing.

"They're making more spears so we can't wait them out," he said at last. "Whatever they are. Wherever they've come from. They're too smart, and they want our scalps for some reason."

Shoulders rising and falling quickly, Casey nodded again to show she was listening.

Realizing there was only one thing to do, Jonas looked across at his daughter. His gaze was soft but resilient, his demeanor committed. "I'm injured. I won't be able to keep up."

Casey stared at him a moment, then felt her lips curl down and hot tears run down her cheeks. "Dad…"

"Give me your gun."

Casey watched him load it for her from one of his black pouches.

"Silver bullets," he said, and Casey's eyes filled with hope as she took back the gun.

"Maybe enough, maybe not," he continued, tying one of his pouches on her belt. "So I'm going to charge them, kill as many as I can."

"I'm sorry!" Casey stammered. "You said take the knives! I should have listened! I should have checked! I'm sorry!"

"This is not your fault," her father whispered, hugging her as best he could through the branches. "Hit or not hit. It would still be the same plan. It's not your fault. It's mine. The knives are like you said, for close combat. And there are too many of them. I should have brought more silver bullets, especially for you; it's just been so long since…" Jonas shook his head. "I thought we were safe now. But I should have realized if unicorns were coming through, that maybe something bad would come too."

Casey quieted, still shaking her head from side to side.

"Hey," her father added suddenly, lightening his tone and reaching out to shake her shoulder. "This ain't no sacrifice. This is a plan. We've got a big range advantage, and once they realize we have more weapons that can kill them, the fear will come, and when it does, there's a good chance they'll break and retreat and I'll get away too. But no matter what happens, I want you to run home and not look back and wait for me there. Promise me."

"I promise," Casey croaked.

Jonas reached over and wiped her tears away. "I need you to be strong. Strong like you were when you saved the horse last night."

Casey almost blurted out, *That was different! There were voices in my head!* Yet some part of her knew how crazy that would sound, and crazy was not what her father needed to hear just then, so she nodded silently instead.

"Good," Jonas said. Then he fixed his gaze on the reptilian pack. "The moment you hear the first shot, you go."

Casey nodded.

"The moment you hear the first shot, you go," her father repeated without looking at her.

Casey's chin rose up. "First shot. Ready."

Jonas smiled, and a tear his daughter did not see rolled down his weathered cheek. Perhaps to himself or perhaps to Casey, he said, "It's going to be loud. Chaotic. A total surprise." Jonas swung his legs around, ready to shimmy out of the tree as fast as he could. "This is going to work. You're going to make it home, and hell, I'm a great shot. Take out that little blue-beaned trail boss first, and I wouldn't be surprised if—"

A mournful whistle rose in the woods, cutting him off: *Wrreee! Wrreee! Wrrreee!*

Every living thing that heard it stilled and looked for the source. Then a carved white staff, whirling with the blurring speed of hummingbird wings, rose up into the sky. After reaching its apex, some twenty-five feet above the ground, the staff inexplicably stayed aloft, hovering under its own power, steadily singing its woeful, eerie song.

Every nearby eye, lizard, human or otherwise, was drawn to it and watched its flight.

"What…what is that?" Casey asked, wiping matted strands of nut-brown hair from her eyes. "It sounds like—"

"Taliko…" her father said with obvious relief. "Finally."

Casey's next question was cut short by a crashing crescendo rushing toward them through the trees. Several teeth rattling moments after it had begun, a large bouncing rock came tumbling out of the woods toward the lizards. Seeing one side was flattened, much like it had been shaved with a saw, she silently amended herself, *Half a rock.*

"Casey, listen to me," her father said in a rush. "Hold on tight, close your eyes and cover your ears as best you can. Hurry Casey! Do it! Do it n—"

Casey tightened her grip on the branches nearest her with one hand and moved to cover an ear with the other. Mesmerized as she was by the thundering disc, she was slow. Way, way too slow.

With a final jolt off a half-buried boulder, the careening leather-backed disc bounced high into the air. Casey's eyes rose to follow it, full of wonder as it arced toward the still-spinning staff.

Just as the two were about to collide, a saber-toothed alligator face burst from the disc, followed quickly by hands, feet, and a tail.

Casey's jaw dropped so suddenly she didn't even have time to gasp.

The creature snatched the swirling staff out of the air with one clawed hand and then landed with the sound and fury of an Olympian thunderbolt.

Thwammm!

The rugged canopy on the creature's back shuddered with the impact.

Immediately, as if awakened by the vibration, a smoky topaz glow arose beneath the shell's lowest scales.

It's a giant turtle! Casey realized, watching the light spiral swiftly to the shell top and sparkle in its gemstone eyes.

Fully illuminated, the shell blinked three times; two quick heartbeats, *thrump-thrump*, followed by a devastating thunderclap.

Bursting forth like a rampaging tsunami, the mind-numbing shockwave expanded in all directions, indiscriminately bludgeoning everything around its epicenter for nearly fifty feet.

First dazed by the concussive blast and then razed by the biting edge of the sonic wave tearing at every inch of exposed skin, Casey reeled from the magical two-pronged assault.

The lizardmen didn't stand a chance.

Scattered like rag dolls, most of them helplessly rode the surge until they struck one of the thicker trees or a heavy stone and were smashed senseless.

Surrounded by the earsplitting cracks and ponderous crashes of trees rent well beyond their breaking point, Casey gritted her teeth against the pain and locked her hands together, praying that the tree she was in wouldn't share that sundering fate.

Thankfully, the sonic assault faded as its blast radius grew.

Woozy from the thunderclap, Casey rocked back and forth, trying to open her eyes. When her eyelids finally did flicker open, the stinging light of day made her vision hazy and watery.

Her heavy head drooped—and drooped again.

Midswoon Casey realized she was losing her perch in the tree. Gripped by the sudden terror of being torn apart by the revolting lizards below, Casey opened her mouth to cry out to her father but couldn't find her voice.

Instead, her eyelids fluttered closed with the effort, consciousness slipped away, and she fell.

Though but a third of the lizardmen remained conscious enough to get back on their feet, these rushed the alligator-faced turtle with reckless abandon.

Taliko reacted instantly, whirling and twirling his dirge-singing bo-staff until all eight of the remaining creatures had joined their brothers lying in the dirt. The brief skirmish came and went without him being nicked even once by fang or claw, though two javelins did clatter harmlessly against the back of his shell.

When the last of the creatures fell, Taliko leaned on his staff, breathing normally and surveying the area for any remaining threats.

"That was very impressive," Jonas said above him, his voice tight and strained. "Now how about a little help here?"

Seeing that the sharpshooter held onto a rigid tree limb with one hand and his dangling, unconscious daughter with the other, Taliko scampered over to them with rabbit-like grace. Casey stirred at the sound of her father's voice and began to wake just as the turtle arrived and lifted his hands to catch the precious cargo.

"Here she comes," Jonas said.

Jolted fully alert by the drop and catch, Casey looked into Taliko's glittering gemstone eyes and sucked a startled breath through her teeth.

"Dad?" she called out hopefully.

Jonas landed with a grunt beside them just as the turtle set her back on her feet.

"Casey," he said as if they'd run into someone in town. "I want you to meet Taliko."

Casey turned to look at her father. "You're…friends with a seven-foot-tall talking turtle and never told me?"

"We don't see each other often," her father replied.

"And whose fault is that?" the massive turtle mumbled.

"Hey," Jonas said defensively. "I stop by the Lookout all the time."

"Hrrmmpphh." the turtle rolled his topaz eyes.

"It's not my fault you're always sleeping. You get my gifts don't you?"

"What? You mean those sickly chickens and half-dead cows?"

"Chickens?" Casey wondered out loud. "So they don't run off?"

Jonas's jaw dropped. "Sickly? Half-dead? Why, you ungrateful mollusk. Just where were you anyway? That was a pretty close call just—"

"Hold it, hold it, hold it!"

Casey's screech silenced both man and reptile, but when her father and Taliko turned to look at her, the questions tangled in her throat. "You two! What is? How? Where did?"

Casey threw her hands up and howled in frustration.

Jonas and Taliko, flooded suddenly with postbattle giddiness, looked at each other and started laughing.

Casey, however, who had had her entire world upended in the last twenty-four hours, was well beyond merriment of any kind. Mistaking their relief for amusement, she never felt the anger rising in her heart and just released it. Eyes blazing, teeth bared, Casey sprinted at her father and slammed him on the chest with both fists. Jonas, unprepared for the assault, felt the air leave his lungs and staggered backward several feet, gasping. She turned next on the giant turtle, but the saber teeth looming above her head gave Casey pause, and so she simply waved her fists at him and pretended to push him away.

"Ugh!" she thundered, pacing back and forth with every shout. "Magic horses! Voices in my head! Walking, talking turtles! *What?* Is going on?"

The silence lingered.

"Well, you're in trouble," Taliko said matter-of-factly. "I'm going—"

"Nowhere thunderclap," Casey snarled. "You ain't going nowhere! Not till I get some answers."

Taliko's gaze slid over to Jonas. "Sounds just like her mother."

Casey's eyes burst out of her head. "You knew my mother?"

The turtle's bo-staff twirled and then struck the ground with a meaty *whump.*

"I did," Taliko nodded once. "She is my Maker, and entrusted me to watch over you, which I have done since you slept in a basket."

"Maker?" Casey's jaw fell. "Slept in a basket?" Tears running down her cheeks, she turned back to her father. "Dad? Please?"

"Okay, okay," Jonas answered softly. "How long have you been hearing voices?"

"Just last night," Casey brushed her eyes. "I thought it was the horse. That's why I went out to help him."

Taliko lifted his head higher. "Definitely one of the herd that was here yesterday. It must have gotten separated somehow and left behind. I was out looking for evidence of their purpose when you came under attack, but had no success in finding their trail even where I knew it should be."

"I saw them too," Casey told Taliko, "but he doesn't have a horn like the others."

"A juvenile," her father said thoughtfully. "Mustn't have come in yet. He's in our barn now, waiting for us to return with some of this fruit for his injuries. At least I think he is."

"Hmm," Taliko intoned. "This could be a very unfortunate thing, I think."

"What? Why?" Jonas and Casey asked at the same time.

"First needs tended first. You two must get back, and I will..." Taliko looked about the clearing. "Decide what must be done here. Soon, I shall be finished and meet you at your nest. There is much to discuss when I arrive."

Taliko looked at Jonas. "It would be wise for you to tell her the truths she should already know along the way."

Jonas nodded.

5

CARDS ON THE TABLE

When Point Lookout appeared through the trees ahead of them, Casey vented her frustration.

"Dad!" she shouted into the sky.

"I know, I know," he said. "I just don't know where to begin."

A few steps later, Jonas wheeled around, abruptly got down on one knee, and took Casey's hand. "You weren't born in Texas. You were born…" Jonas looked down, took a deep breath, and looked up again. "Let me start over. You never lived in Texas. You have always lived in our house, right here under Thunder Peak. And it's always been your house and our house because…"

"Because?" Casey prompted him.

Jonas looked her in the eye. "Because I've always been your father."

Casey stared at him blankly.

"The story about the stagecoach attack is just that, a story," Jonas continued. "A lie I had to make up to hide the truth about your mother."

Casey whispered, "You're my real father?"

Jonas nodded.

Tears began to fall out of Casey's eyes like broken snowflakes, each one of them a bullet of fear that found Jonas's heart.

When Casey just stared at him, Jonas perceived resentment and disappointment and felt a heavy cloak of despair wrap him around the shoulders.

"I'm sorry about lying to you all these years," he began hoarsely, "but once you know everything, I hope you'll—"

Casey rushed in, knocking free the tears Jonas had been holding back with a fierce hug.

"I'm so glad," Casey sobbed. "I've always felt so guilty about loving you more than the people in that picture."

In many ways father and daughter clung to each other then for the very first time. Her words meant the world to him because Jonas always felt Casey might think the opposite, that he had failed to live up to what she thought of the brave people in the picture. Eyes still closed, Jonas basked in the feeling of having released the burden of the lie, but also knew it was just the beginning and there was a lot more of the story to tell.

A few moments later, Casey realized it too. "So where…where is mom? Was she an Indian? What happened to her? Is she…" Casey trailed off, fearing that in gaining a father, she was about to lose a mother again.

"As far as I know"—Jonas came to his feet—"she's fine. Just very far away."

"Why isn't she here?"

Jonas clenched his daughter's hand, his grip emphasizing what he said next. "You need to understand, that wherever she is right now, she loves you and always has, and thinks of you often."

"But why *isn't* she here? Did she leave us?"

A tidal thrumming rose up in the woods around them, cutting off whatever

Jonas was about to say. Both of them knew they should recognize the sound, but the racket arose so suddenly that their thoughts were paralyzed.

The first hornet flew passed Jonas's nose, and he stepped back in panicked surprise. "Angry hive. We better rabbit along," he said, and the pair began to trot down the trail. Right around the next bend, they plunged headlong into a menacing swarm harassing a brown bear pillaging its hive.

"Oh boy," Jonas said. "Not that way." And the pair quickly shuffled off the game trail into the woods.

Risking a quick look back, Casey saw the swarm gather into a frightening cloud of chaotic rage and gruzzz after them.

"It's following us!" she yelled over the violent thrum. "Why is it following us instead of attacking the bear? Ow!" she shouted, stung for the first time.

"I don't know," Jonas grunted, limping as fast as he could. "We'll never make it home. Lots of ponds in these woods—maybe we can find one deep enough."

There were hornets on his clothes, and the fourth or fifth had already stung him. Glancing at his daughter he saw a black cloud of hornets whizzing around her, most of them ready to attack but seemingly held in check by some unseen force.

Heeding her father's words Casey took in the passing trees, assessing their location, and realized suddenly that one of her favorite watering holes was nearby.

"Follow me!" she called back over her shoulder.

Casey had dubbed the spot Arrowhead Pond after the pointy diving rock perfectly situated at the edge of the deeper end. It was maybe a quarter mile off, and Casey ran like the wind, forcing Jonas to call out numerous times for her to slow down, but even uninjured he wouldn't have been able to keep up with her.

Seven black bells! Jonas swore silently. *First time in forever I don't wear my moccasins out here, and this is what I get.*

The bees surged after them and soon Jonas was getting stung at every step.

He pushed on through the pain. Then his vision began to blur. Knowing he'd die where he lay if he stumbled and fell, Jonas dug deeper. Dug down into the well forged during the agonies of the Civil War, and somehow kept his legs moving until finally the leaves parted and the pond appeared before him. Dropping the apples and his gun belt next to Casey's, he leaped into the cool, refreshing water with a shout and stayed submerged until his lungs ached more than the stings.

The massive swarm was a marvel to see, pulsing and churning and, inexplicably, seemingly determined to wait them out. Each time one of them took a breath, the hornets dove at them with their vicious stingers.

Fully clothed as they were, Jonas and Casey could not tread water for very long. The moment she thought it, her father surfaced and shouted as fast as he could before ducking under again, "We won't last this way; we have to strip or drown."

Casey nodded her head, but even as she clutched at the first button, the voice from the previous night returned: "I am here! Remove yourselves from the water, and I shall carry you both to safety!"

"Dad wait!" Casey shouted. "Follow me!"

Jonas cried back, "Casey no! We'll—" but stopped in midshout as the colt from the barn jumped majestically over the pond and quickly turned back to wait for them at the water's edge. "Right then! Go! Go! Go!"

Jonas was shocked to see the maddened hornets coalesce around the new target like a starving beast but gratefully used the reprieve to collect their gun belts and the saddlebag full of ice apples for which they had suffered so much already.

Jonas struggled with his injured thigh and the lack of a stirrup, forcing the horse to endure an endless barrage of stings. Once he was finally aboard, Jonas hoisted Casey up easily and the colt launched into the woods.

"Stay low," Jonas gritted, burying his face into the horse's mane to ward off the bees and even deadlier branches. Casey did the same in her father's back but needn't have worried—despite the injuries he'd incurred the night before and the mounting stings all over his body, the steed unerringly wound around trees and over rocks and scrub until the swarm fell behind.

With the pain of the stings added to that of his injured thigh, Jonas wheezed, hissed, and winced through the entire ride, especially at the quicker turns and landings. Nor was he ever sure when the stinging ceased. At some point a shadow fell over him, and he knew they were back in the safety of the barn at last.

Casey dismounted and ran to the doors.

The gruzzz outside was growing quickly, so quickly that Casey grimaced with dire certainty that hornets were going to get into the barn before she sealed it up.

After closing the right-hand side door, she dashed to the left and risked a glance outside.

The hornets were stopped some ten feet away, the swarm rolling and tumbling in space like a pent-up storm cloud.

Keen to seize on their good fortune, she started to tug the door closed.

Then she saw the face.

A wolf's face, full of fangs, in the swarm—the very same giant fangs she used to see in her nightmares!

Impossible! Casey stumbled back.

Wait! Casey squinted. *A trick! It's just a trick. Shadows and clouds will look like anything if you let them.*

Despite that apparent truth, Casey remained frozen.

Close it! Close it! she yelled at herself, over and over, but the mesmerizing fear held her fast until the face abruptly disappeared.

With a final shake of the head, she cleared away the last of the fear, then slammed closed the barn door and leaned back against it in relief.

Just hornets, she told herself as the gruzzz outside diminished. *Just hornets.*

The barn filled with the sound of heavy breathing, human and horse.

Jonas tried to dismount, but disoriented and sapped of his strength, he simply fell and landed with a heavy thud.

"Dad!" Casey ran over to help him.

Jonas rolled over onto his back with a groan while the horse cantered softly away.

Taking Casey's hand, Jonas pulled himself up to one knee, gasping. "How many stings?"

"Half a dozen or so I reckon," Casey replied, wincing as she looked over the welts covering his face and neck. "You?"

Jonas had suffered over a dozen stings in the first minute and could guess why his daughter hadn't. More uncertain was why not a single hornet had pursued them into the barn. But all that would have to wait. "A lot more than that," he grunted. "I feel like I'm on fire."

"This is the first time I've ever been stung," she added, taking the heavy bag from his shoulder and helping him up to his feet.

Jonas looked at the horse. "Thank you," he said, then swayed as if he was about to lose consciousness.

"Dad!" Casey slipped a strong, wiry arm around him. "You've got to lie down and rest."

Casey peered through the doors to be certain the swarm had moved off.

"Let's hurry in case they come back," she said and then bore the weight of her father and the saddlebag all the way back to the house without even realizing how easily she'd done it.

The young stallion watched the Earthers go, its glistening black coat pocked by countless, burning hornet stings. Once they were safely inside, the steed glanced around, looking about for the protection it sensed at hand but with no idea in what form it might be.

Occupied thus, a sudden bolt of agony struck him without warning over the eyes and he shook his head until it passed.

He had no idea if the others would come back for him, or how long that might even take, but the pain at the top of his head told him that if they didn't come soon, it wouldn't matter if they ever did.

Inside the house Casey guided her father to the sofa and fetched the soothing oils and lotions they kept on hand for hurts and blisters. After tending to the welts and cleaning and dressing the gash in his thigh, she mixed and warmed herbal remedies and helped him drink them while he tried not to move.

In time he fell into a tormented sleep, mumbling about secrets, how beautiful Casey's mother had been and how much he missed her. How it had been so many years, longer than the war even, but now maybe there was hope.

"Hope for what?" Casey wondered quietly from a seat not too far away. Then her thoughts fell into an endless array of questions: *And what was that he said about caves and silver bullets?* It seemed important, but now she couldn't remember it. *And how had he known about the silver, anyway? What kind of creatures were those lizards? Why didn't their mere existence shock him like it did her?*

Taliko. She nodded. *That's why.* Casey gasped. Was her mother a witch to send a creature like that to watch over her? *Does that make me a witch?* Casey chewed her bottom lip. *Was she evil? Like in-the-bible evil?*

With that thought, Casey thought it best to stop pondering and glanced over at the sofa.

Her father continued to languish in immense pain, full of welts and drifting in and out of wakefulness. She looked at her own arms then to see her bruises were nearly gone.

That doesn't make me evil, she thought. *It just makes me a fast healer.*

Grasping that thought, Casey felt the energy drain suddenly from her body and began to yawn. Having gotten little sleep herself the previous night, it was only a matter of minutes before she too slipped into a fitful slumber.

Sometime later Casey woke, certain there had been a noise but uncertain what it was.

It came again: a heavy staccato clack at the door.

Swiftly and silently, she retrieved her Navy from its holster, tucked a silver knife in her belt, and took up position at the side of the door.

Casey opened her mouth, and the voice that came out was so devoid of the fear she felt the night before that it surprised her: "Who is it?"

A gravelly whisper replied, "Taliko."

Casey exhaled in relief and unbolted the door.

The massive turtle turned sideways and slipped in on clawed feet, his steps lighter and bouncier than Casey would have imagined.

The image sparked a memory from years ago—Casey asking her father why their door was so big and wide. He had replied then that he just liked it that way. Now, abruptly, she knew that to be a falsehood. The door had been enlarged to accommodate Taliko.

Upon seeing Jonas lying on the sofa, Taliko's face tilted sharply. "What has happened?" he asked, gemstone eyes examining him from head to toe.

Casey, having gathered herself a bit from all that had happened, sat down on the edge of the couch and continued a subtle inspection of the giant turtle while she told him the story of the hornet attack, noting how his shell was dark brown, almost black, but his thick skin was several shades lighter, like a deer's, then lighter still in his vital areas, like sand.

"That is very curious indeed," Taliko observed. "I know of some leaves and plants growing nearby that can help. I shall fetch them and return shortly."

The floorboards creaked under Taliko's weight as he moved toward the door. Once he got there, he paused and turned. "I checked on the steed before coming here. He suffers as well and is quite hungry. Perhaps you can bring him some of the ice apples."

"Uhm…sure. Much obliged. I'll do that."

Taliko opened the door, and Casey sprang to her feet, "Wait? What? Did you just say the steed? You mean you *think* he's hungry or…you spoke to him?"

"'Spoke' perhaps, is not the right word." Taliko looked out toward the barn. "'Communicated' would be more precise."

"Communicated." Casey echoed the brawny reptile.

Taliko nodded again. "Apparently there are many tales that need passage. I am looking forward to their telling on my return."

"Me too…" Casey whispered.

She watched him disappear into the dark woods, then closed the door and slid the bolt home with a reassuring thud.

Casey checked on her father, adjusting his pillows and changing some of the leaves covering his welts. Finished, she sat on the edge of the sofa again and saw that he seemed to be resting easier.

I suppose he'll be fine if I just poke out to the barn for a short spell.

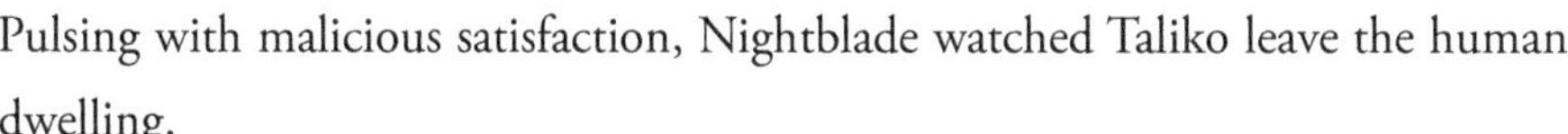

Pulsing with malicious satisfaction, Nightblade watched Taliko leave the human dwelling.

Maneuvered now into a position to infiltrate the mind of the shell warrior—the scaled folk had proved their usefulness. More, they had warned him that the juvenile and the half breed shared a mind-speak bond—how else could the unicorn have known she needed assistance with the honey collectors?

Finding the bear had been fortunate. But fortune favors the prepared and was to be both expected and welcomed. Though it had proven too stubborn to influence for long, the animal was easy enough to agitate into striking the hive. Once aroused, the honey collectors were more easily driven, and even now their tiny, lifeless bodies lay in the woods, each drop of mane-folk blood devoured from their stingers.

Assured thus that his frein had been well spent, Nightblade watched the shell warrior disappear into the woods. Oh, how he longed for the moment he would dismember the foul jevaling and see it fade away into ethereal dust.

Patience.

Manipulate from the shadows.

The moment to strike must be both prepared and prepared for.

Let the juvenile regain its strength. Each time it left the barn, Nightblade would instigate more honey collectors to strike, then recover the blood spoils when it was over.

The process would take time. Hopefully not too much time.

If only human folk blood wasn't so toxic. Then he might have manipulated the destruction of the half breed long ago and restored himself. As it was, human blood tainted the inherent blood magic of faerie beings whenever the two were mixed, making it useless to any creature that might feed on it, including him. The same uselessness was inherent for jevaled beings; the magic that evolved them dissipated when it left their bodies.

No matter. The plan proceeded apace and as well as could be expected.

One spikeless unicorn, one half breed, a jevaled shell warrior, and one human, even armed with silver as they were, would be no match for the Cree Chieftain once he was reborn.

6
FORBIDDEN

"Hello?"

Though she had been sleeping soundly, Taliko's visit had set her thoughts racing, and now she was simply too alert to fall asleep again. Looking to her father, she watched him resting for some twenty minutes before deciding it was okay to simply let him be, light a lantern, and head over to the barn.

Now here she was, stepping into the gloom with the heavy satchel full of ice apples over her shoulder. "Hello?" she called again.

A gentle hoof clop sounded in the darkness, and the outlines of a horse came into view.

"There you are," she said, reaching up to stroke his face. "You were very brave, coming for us like that. How did you even know we were in trouble?"

The horse stepped into the light, then nudged the saddlebag with his nose, and Casey got a good look at the endless angry bruises added to the bites and scratches the steed had suffered the previous night.

"Oh, you poor thing," she said, reaching into the bag and pulling out a piece of fruit. "Dad said this is just the thing."

The horse stepped back, nodding its head sharply.

"What's the matter?" Casey asked, still holding out the fruit.

The horse trod slowly forward and then back each time Casey tried to feed it the fruit. After several failed attempts to get the horse to eat, she let the horse nuzzle her hand until finally he pushed it against her chest.

"What?" Casey held the fruit to her mouth. "You want me to eat it?"

The horse pawed the ground and knocked the fruit against her face with his muzzle.

"Ow." Casey winced. "My tooth. All right. All right." Casey bit into the small, delicious fruit, and not realizing how hungry she was, devoured it quickly, followed by another. The horse, with its luminous silver eyes, watched her all the while, as if waiting.

Tired of standing, Casey sat on a milking bench and pulled out a third. "These were supposed to be for you," she said, taking another bite, but if you're not going to—

"Hello."

"Finally!" Casey exclaimed. "Why do you keep giving me the silent treatment? It makes me feel like I'm going crazy."

"For that, I apologize," the steed said in her mind. "But I had to be sure of your motivations."

"Motivations?" Casey muttered. "I'm trying to help you."

"And for doing just so, I thank you," the horse said, taking an apple from her hand. "Still, I was told there would be no Sentinels here, so I am surprised to find you. And when you finally did answer my call, you were wielding a firestick, so I chose to exercise caution. Have you been stranded as well? Does anyone know you're here, hiding among the humans?"

"Sentinel? I'm not—I don't even know what that is."

Casey squinted in bewilderment as the horse finished a second apple. Peering at her closely, his thoughts asked, "You are not a Sentinel? Then why are you here?"

"I live here, with my dad." Casey giggled softly. "Who's now my father," she added happily.

The horse raised his head sideways. Casey could sense his confusion and continued. "I thought he was my uncle. That he adopted me after my parents died so he could raise me like a dad, but now I just found out that he really *is* my father." Casey looked up into the horse's silver eyes. "I have you to thank for that. So, thank you."

The horse continued to stare at her a moment, then his voice appeared in her mind again. "But we communicate—that should be impossible for a human. You have a jevaled ally. And this place." The steed glanced around the barn. "The wards are so powerful around it that I sensed it as an aril haven from a great distance…"

The horse trailed off for a moment, then mused, "And yet, though you hear my words in your mind, I don't hear yours unless you say them aloud…"

Peering intently at Casey, the horse tilted its head, first left, then right.

Abruptly, its eyes widened, gaze filling with a realization that drained the enthusiasm from its movements. "The human is your sire…Now I understand why communication has been so difficult between us. I thought it was because I have yet to go through my Wrivening. But that was false. It is you, and what you must be—one of the Forbidden."

"Forbidden?" Casey frowned. "I don't know anything about no Forbidden. What's that mean? It sounds…ugly."

The barn door opened then, and Jonas shuffled in with Taliko. "What sounds ugly?" her father asked.

"You're up!" Casey said. "You should be resting!"

"And miss the excitement?" her father said with a chuckle. "Not a chance. I'll be okay. Taliko gave me something awful to drink, does a lot for the pain."

Casey nodded. "Well, I'm glad you're here now. Both of you," she added, glancing at Taliko, and the turtle nodded at her. She smiled at him and then turned back to the horse. "He called me one of the Forbidden, whatever that means. But I don't like the sound of it."

Jonas watched the horse nuzzle an apple out of the bag and eat it. "So you can really talk to this horse? Is the fruit helping?"

Casey nodded, then clarified. "Well, I can talk to him, but it's…I can hear him in my head, but he only hears me if I talk out loud, if that makes sense."

Casey looked at her father and saw him staring at her intently, his expression unreadable. Worrying suddenly how her words sounded, she quickly added, "I'm not crazy! You know a giant talking turtle! And he can talk to the horse too! Ask him!"

Jonas took a seat on the milking bench to take the weight off his injured thigh. "I don't think you're crazy," he said, raising his hand. "No, I'm just trying to make sense of what's going on. What it all means."

"Okay," Casey took a deep breath and nodded.

"How come I can see him?" Jonas asked. "Didn't you say Nash and Savannah couldn't see them?"

"Huh?" Casey wondered aloud before turning to the steed. "Why can my dad see you when my friends couldn't?"

After a long moment of consideration, the steed replied, "Invisibility is an innate defense possessed by all unicorns to use at will. The magic works best against creatures bred of shadow and darkness. But it is also very strong against those who lack a faerie bloodline—such as humans. At the moment, I am also not trying to be unseen."

Casey translated. Jonas nodded, glancing at her as if expecting a question. When it was obvious she hadn't put the facts together yet, he gestured toward the sack of ice apples on the floor. "Right then. Toss me one of those before he eats them all."

Casey did as he asked while the horse watched. After glancing up at the horse a moment, Casey nodded and turned back to her father as he took his first bite. "He says it's not the fruit. You won't be able to hear him unless you are one of the Forbidden too."

"Figured as much," Jonas said around a mouthful. "Damn near forgot how good these are. I'm eating it anyway."

"These are even better than our apples," Casey said frankly. "The way the juice tingles like cold water is amazing."

"It certainly is," Jonas agreed. "That's why I named them ice apples."

"You named them?"

"Long story for another time," Jonas said, taking a loud bite.

"So these have been out there all along? Why haven't we ever gotten any?"

Jonas sighed. "The waiting. It's always been about the waiting for me."

"Waiting for what?"

"I'm not sure how to answer that," Jonas said sadly. "Your mom showed me that tree, said the fruit was special. That it could heal and nourish her frein."

"Frein?" Casey asked.

Jonas nodded. "Her soul, her spirit. I think that was just her word for it. But harvesting from the pearlwood was a big reason her people used to come here. That's why I thought it might help him." Jonas gestured at the horse. "And I never ate from it, so there would always be plenty if..." Jonas shook his head. "I've been waiting for her to come back again, so I look in on it occasionally to see if it looks picked, or for some other sign that might mean she could be returning soon."

"Ahh." Casey breathed, her gaze drifting up the walls of the barn but looking into the past. "A sign, like something that couldn't be explained. Something like this horse."

"Something like this horse." Jonas agreed, and Casey grew reflective, watching them both eat while Taliko hunkered down close to the ground, alertly surveying all with his watchful topaz eyes.

It was a lot to absorb. Still, Jonas knew Casey would make the connections and break the silence once she was ready, and she did. "Dad, do you know what a Forbidden is?"

"I think I do," he answered. "Come closer."

Casey did so, and Jonas took her hand. "Your mother lives where this horse does. She used to visit me often, and even though she still wants to, the people in charge there won't let her come back. According to the Elders or some such, falling in love with a human is against the law. Forbidden. And us having children, like you, was especially forbidden. So that's what I think it means."

While he spoke hot tears filled Casey's eyes, and she was already hugging him before he finished.

"I'm sorry Nightingale," Jonas whispered, rubbing her back. "I wish it were a happier story than that, but the most important thing to remember is"—Jonas dropped his eyes a moment and then looked back up—"is that love doesn't care about time or distance. That's how strong it can be, and forbidden or not, no one can stop us from how we feel. And from that came you, and a true blessing you are if ever there was one. Wherever she is right now, I know she feels the same way and she's glad you're here safe with me."

Casey stepped back. "Safe from who?"

"From them. Those idiot Elders. To them, our relationship was a crime, so your mother risked everything to get you here."

"If I was born across the ocean or wherever, how did I get here? How did mom?" Casey looked at the unicorn. "How did he get here?"

"All of you came the same way. You though, were quite a puzzle at first," Jonas admitted quietly. "I was asleep when a loud bang downstairs at the door woke me—a real thud, like someone was trying to kick it in. I checked from the second-floor windows, but it was the middle of the night, and couldn't see anything or anyone.

"I crept down, quiet like, with Liberty tight against my shoulder. That's when I saw it."

"Saw what?" Casey asked, eyes wide.

Jonas smiled before continuing. "A basket. In the middle of the floor."

"Me?" Casey asked.

Jonas nodded. "You. Tiny little you. Wrapped in a gold blanket. And no telling how you were dropped off with the door locked and no window broke."

Casey's eyes sparkled. She glanced over at the mysterious horse, then Taliko, and finally back to her father. This, she realized suddenly, was the story she had been waiting her whole life for.

"I opened up and called out a few times to see if anyone was about. Later I found out your mom sent you here with Taliko to protect you. But he wasn't ready to introduce himself yet and didn't answer. So I sat down to have a look at you. That's when I saw you had little moccasins on your feet. Just like mine."

Casey looked down at her toes.

Jonas nodded. "The very same. They just keep growing right along with you. Under your blanket I found the hawk pendant that I gave you for your tenth birthday."

It is part of the secret! Casey felt a pleasant tingle run through her body and hugged herself. *I knew it!*

Jonas brushed his face quickly, then finished. "That was all the evidence I needed. No question. Somehow, someway, your mom found a way to get you to me, where she knew you'd be safe and cared for."

Casey smiled at him and then peered back at her feet again, at the magic moccasins that she could never grow out of. In the midst of wriggling her toes, Casey's face darkened, and her eyes snapped up. "Do you think they hurt her? Punished her? Is she all right?"

"Punished, yeah. But hurt her? No, I don't think they hurt her," Jonas said with certainty. "When we realized she was pregnant, we started to plan. Next time she came, I was going to sell the place so we could move somewhere they'd never find us. Only you made it, so they must have found out somehow. It was dire straits trouble for sure, that's all that could have kept her, but your mom is tough. Really tough. That's where you get your spirit from, that fire in your heart, and she was ready for whatever punishment she thought they might give her."

Casey frowned. "Wish I could go wherever she is and bring them Elders the trouble they deserve."

"Me too."

They were quiet a moment, and the horse whinnied softly, eating another ice apple out of the satchel.

"Wait a second," Casey said, pointing at the horse. "He said something like that too. Falling in love with a human? What does that mean?"

Jonas chuckled. "I was starting to think you weren't getting it."

"Noo," Casey searched for the words that would clarify her thoughts. "It's just, I always imagined there was just one secret. But really there are a bunch of them, and all of them lead to new questions about more secrets. So the whole thing is like a great big, out of control fire. And I'm trying to get there so fast with the water that I lose half the bucket on the way to putting it out."

Jonas nodded knowingly, and after a few moments of listening to the great black colt munching on apples, he began. "You look like her. Thin. You've even got those cute angles to your chin and nose like she does. The narrow diamond-shaped ears. Quick and strong. And getting stronger I bet." Jonas nodded in memory and snickered. "Your mom was stronger than any man I ever met. I can't imagine how powerful the men are where she lives."

Casey shook her head. "Why do you keep saying it like that? Where does she live?"

"Your mom, the horses you saw, this horse right here. They live…in another place. They can only come here through a special gate. It's hidden in the forest out past Point Lookout. I don't know how it works, but it's like…If we had a magic door right here in this barn, and when you walked through, you'd come out in town. And if you were in town and walked back through the same door the other way, you would return here, in the barn."

"I kept thinking you meant another country." Casey tossed her long braid with a side to side shake of the head. "But that sounds…sounds like the rabbit hole in *Alice in Wonderland.*"

Jonas chuckled. "I haven't read that one yet, but my guess is you're probably right."

Casey giggled with him. "So much has changed since yesterday."

"It has," her father nodded.

After a long glance at the colt, her father continued. "Apparently, according to your mother, her people were good friends with the Apache and other Indians before the whites came and ruined it for them. No way to know for sure of course, but it occurred to me after, a lot after, that her people coming through the portal, befriending Indians, and doing amazing things like talking to animals could be the source of a lot of legends."

"Okay, that sort of does make sense," Casey conceded. "Wait! You think that's why everyone thinks Thunder Peak is haunted?"

"I do." Jonas pointed at her. "Because that's where the unpredictable weather comes from. Thunder Peak makes its own magic. Something even your mom and her people don't understand. But loose magic up in the sky opens sky doors that allow the storms to pass back and forth like they're coming out of nowhere. And why sometimes we hear thunder and have rain when there's no clouds at all."

"Loose magic." Casey echoed him softly.

"Loose magic." Her father nodded. "Old Hickory calls it spirit magic. We call it ghosts and the devil's work. But that's the real reason, even if I don't explain it very well."

"Whoa..."

"Whoa," Jonas agreed. "So your mom called herself an aril, not a human. She said, in her...realm, I think it was—but she also said kingdom and homeland, but that was rather like we say country. Anyway, they think very little of us humans over there for some reason. So that plays into the Forbidden thing too.

"Aril," Casey mused, glancing around the barn. Her eyes wandered for a long moment, then widened suddenly and snapped back to her father like a whip. "What's mom's name?" she asked.

"Riell," Jonas answered. "Her name is Riell. But I called her Mae, because that's when I met her, in the spring, and it was a long time before we spoke to each other and learned each other's names."

"Rye-el." Casey rolled the name over her tongue. "That's pretty. But why even have a law against arils loving humans?" she asked wonderingly. "What difference does it make?"

"That I don't know." Jonas shook his head sadly. "She just told me there was a law, and I never really got around to asking her why."

Silence fell in the barn. After a time a soft snort and whinny caught Casey's attention. "The fruit of the snowbark is kindling your faerie blood; with it your words become clearer to me. Your question I have heard. Why the aril shun Earther, and why your mare is not allowed to return is a tale I can tell if your sire cannot."

"Dad!" Casey turned to Jonas. "He said he knows! He can tell us why aril can't marry humans!"

"Right then." Jonas shifted on the milking bench again. "Tell him let's have it."

And thus the unicorn's tale began.

"The magic door you speak of is but one of many. Together we call them the Tyndryn Trailway, and only the aril can activate them. They say control is a blood gift from the first makers and original builders, so it is they and only they who can open and close them. This they do according to their whim, or when it suits traditions they've imposed."

Casey, wide-eyed, breathlessly relayed the story to her father.

"As they once did here on Earther, the aril often post Sentinels on each side of a gate. For a time, perhaps a long time, the scouts and the humans who lived nearby worked together in harmony. Something happened. I know not what, exactly, but a battle of some kind erupted during which the Sentinels opened the gate to flee home and were pursued before they could close it again.

"The aril are physically stronger and faster than humans, so until then they had no reason to fear them, even in great numbers. But the humans who came through the gate that fateful day carried with them new weapons that the aril had no defense against—the firestick. Many aril died in that bloody struggle before the humans were defeated and their weapons destroyed. Afterward they abandoned trading with humans entirely and refuse now to open the gate here except on special harvesting occasions.

"To have come here often enough to have fallen in love with your sire, it's likely your mother was a Sentinel of the highest pedigree. I too was on a harvesting expedition when I was stranded. Finding you was an accident. I was trying to distance myself from the fang folk of your realm when I sensed your dwellings; they are surrounded by very powerful wards of protection, probably woven by your mother during one of her missions here. Initially I believed the aril had been lying all along about the Sentinels, but now that I realize what you are, I am amazed you were allowed to survive at all, even here."

Is that why Mae sent Taliko to be her guardian? Jonas wondered. *Was she worried the aril might send someone after Casey?*

"There is no doubt your mare loved you with all her heart, because she certainly risked her life to get you here, a place where she knew the Elders would have no influence over you, and has been punished mightily for her crime."

"That is so mean." Casey shook her head. "Hurting people just because they care about each other and want to have a family. Wait!" Casey's thoughts shifted suddenly, and her eyes filled with concern. "The aril won't come, but they'll let your friends come right? They know you're here. They have to let someone come back to bring *you* home. Don't they?"

The steed looked away and then back again. "They do not. But I believe my family will try to persuade them."

"The aril." Casey sneered. "If only there was something *we* could do."

The steed looked at Casey. "Perhaps there is."

"Really?" Casey stepped forward. "What? Tell me what, and we'll jump to it."

"It is an untried solution, deeply rooted to the heart of your question about why the aril are so hurtful."

"I'd like to know the answer to that too," Jonas said quietly after Casey translated.

"Among the unicorns, we believe the origin of the aril law forbidding nonaril companionship is based on fear. Fear that the blood gift of the original builders will be passed on to the offspring. In this case, to you." The unicorn's silver eyes peered directly at Casey. "And that now you can open the gate without their leave. If the aril fear anything, it is losing mastery of the Tyndryn Trailway. Especially to humans and their firesticks."

Casey finished translating, and overcome suddenly by great mental and physical fatigue, she slumped down into the hay.

Meanwhile, Jonas had grown sullen. This entire tale was not at all what he had been hoping for, and he guessed with some certainty that the appearance of this magical stallion was not the harbinger of his being reunited with Mae. He also got the sense that he was missing something.

Something important.

Taliko stood up shortly after, interrupting all their thoughts. "All of you should be resting now. The moon is long risen, and there is little else to discuss that cannot wait until the new sun."

"Agreed." Jonas rose slowly and helped Casey up. To his daughter he said, "Please thank our new friend for that rescue again, and tell him we'll all talk more in the morning. And if he thinks you can open the gate for him, we'll certainly try, and hopefully help get him home."

Casey did so, and the unicorn whinnied happily to convey his thanks.

Taliko led the way out, followed by father and daughter.

Just after the barn door closed, it creaked open just enough for Casey to slip her head back in. "I don't even know your name," she said. "Mine's Casey. What's yours?"

"Well met Casey," the steed replied with a deep nod. "My name is StarFall."

PART II
SEYCA

7
THE GATEGROVE

Jonas let Casey sleep in the following morning so he could speak with Taliko alone.

"What do you think?" he asked his friend as they strolled through the orchard. Taliko eyed him quietly a moment, and seeing the look, Jonas cut him off before he could start. "I know. Mae's not coming back. I was hoping. Really, really hoping. But this feels all wrong. Like an accident."

"An accident," Taliko echoed him with a gravelly sigh. "Yes, a better description than unfortunate. Don't forget Jonas, I too was hoping to see the Maker again."

Taliko trailed off, wrestling it seemed with his next thought. Jonas waited for him to resume speaking. When he didn't, Jonas asked, "What about StarFall? Do you think someone will come for him?"

Taliko was slow in responding, then finally said, "I am created with the Maker's jevaling magic to help ward over Casey. As such, I have no practical knowledge of unicorn customs. Though it seems certain that they must know he is here. And that calls to mind the many times you have told me about being a soldier. So perhaps honor or duty, if nothing else, will require a rescue attempt."

Jonas thought back to his time in the Confederate Army. "I suppose so, but that was different. That was war. StarFall is trapped and probably feels like a prisoner because he can't get home. But he's not a prisoner of war in need of liberation. He simply fell behind, and they haven't come back for him. Yet. If what he says is true, then his family and friends could be trying frantically to get the aril to reopen the gate. It could happen any time, or never, but…"

"But even if the aril open the gate for the unicorns to return and bring him home, there appears to be little chance of the Maker coming with them," Taliko reflected aloud.

"Exactly." Jonas sighed sadly. "The more I learn about how harsh these aril are, the harder it is to believe that Mae is one of them. Still, we should do our best to get him home. Maybe we can write messages for her, let her know we're all right and that we miss her."

Taliko's stony visage drooped once in agreement. "As you say, but I believe there is more to be considering before embarking—"

A bear lumbered out of the grove, growling grumpily. Jonas and Taliko froze in their tracks, watching him snarl and snap at things they could not see while remaining oblivious to them.

"I think that's the same bear," Jonas said quietly. "The one we saw stirring up the hornets that chased Casey and me back to the barn."

"After the ambush at the pearlwood," Taliko said.

"After the ambush." Jonas echoed him. "Any idea what those…" he fumbled for the correct word. "Lizardmen…were? I thought maybe they come out of the mountain like the others, but these lizards were alive-alive, not dead-alive like the things we fought in there. Casey thinks they're giant whiptails."

"I am in the process of trying to discover just that," Taliko said evenly.

Jonas looked squarely at the stout reptilian. "Process? What process?"

"Communication," Taliko answered, still studying the bear.

"Communication?" Jonas frowned. "One of them is still alive?"

Taliko turned to regard Jonas steadily. "Friend Jonas. They are all but the ones killed during the battle still alive."

Jonas ran his hand down his face and gathered his thoughts. "And you believe this is a good idea?"

Taliko spoke slowly, as he always did. "As it pertains to what you are thinking, and not saying, yes. I feel some kinship with the lizardlings. Once they awoke their demeanor was one of fear and confusion, not aggression. Executing them before learning more about them seemed wrong."

"I don't know Taliko." Jonas shook his head from side to side. "I'm thinking they're from the cave. That it's turning regular animals into monsters again. If not through the gate, where else could they have come from?"

"That is possible," Taliko said firmly. "But the truth is unclear. The cave is too distant to easily check upon, and the lizardlings lack the skills to communicate with me beyond simple sounds and gestures, so it's hard to be sure about anything pertaining them. They are in my nest as we speak."

"How many"

"Eighteen," Taliko replied. "Nine others did not survive; some required mercy."

Jonas nodded and looked into the distance. Then he let out a deep, cleansing breath. "I've seen what you can do Taliko. I trust you to do the right thing. More, I can see now this is a good decision, the right decision. I hope it works out and we get some answers." Jonas sighed. "What happened to me? I used to be more like you, I think. Before the sheriff asked me to dispense justice with my rifle. Or maybe it was before the war."

Jonas paused to rub his wrist across his forehead. "I left Texas, I left my family, looking for peace. Since then I've found many things. A new life. A new love. A couple good friends. And most important, a wonderful daughter. But not peace."

Taliko was quiet a moment, then said, "My life so far teaches me that peace is an illusion. Consider the bear who pillaged the honey from the hornets yesterday, or the fish that he must catch in the stream to eat. The hunting hawks, or even the marauding wolves of Thunder Peak. Together they turn a cycle of life and death that results in harmony. But not peace. I believe what you do for the sheriff is similar. Violence that results in harmony for those who depend on Storm Town. As the instrument of peace for others, you may never have the peace you crave."

Taliko's words made Jonas think of the Colt .45, and how such a gun, or any gun, could be called the Peacemaker. Maybe that was him, he thought with a rueful smile. "Harmony," he said. "I like the sound of that. I can live with that—the way you put it, anyway. That is, long as I get to be the bear and not the fish."

"Just so." Taliko nodded, and together they watched the big brown bear trundle back into the woods, still growling and snarling; at what they could not guess. "I remember when that bear was a cub, have wrestled him many times and watched him grow fine and strong," Taliko observed. "Clear it is to me that something needs be unsettled about him. I shall follow him a bit to see if I can find out what it is. Then check on the lizardlings. Later I will return."

Jonas gave him a wave, and still thinking about the difference between harmony and peace and the role he played in it, he continued his walk. Eventually his thoughts turned back to StarFall and the gate. Once they did, the pang of concern about Casey trying to open it returned, but after tussling with the notion for some time, he still couldn't figure out what it was. Then he recalled that Taliko had seemed about to say something just before the bear arrived and steered the conversation in a new direction.

Making a mental note to revisit what that might be the next time he and Taliko could talk, Jonas left it there and turned his thoughts to the day ahead.

Casey stormed out of the house just after midmorning to find her father working in the grove and StarFall grazing at the side of the barn.

When she reached the bottom of the ladder he was standing on, she looked up, eyes blazing with fury. "What are you doing picking apples?" she demanded. "And why did you let me sleep so late when we have so much work to do trying to open that gate for StarFall?"

Jonas picked a few more apples while his daughter waited, hands on hips, glaring up at him. Deciding he didn't care for her attitude or posture, Jonas dropped the basket of apples he had filled. "Catch" was the only warning he gave.

Casey moved with catlike grace, first side-stepping and then cradling the heavy load before it crashed to the ground. A load every boy her age and most young men would have staggered under.

Jonas plucked one more apple and clenched it in his teeth. Normally he slid down the sides of the ladder with his feet and hands controlling his descent, but his wounded thigh wasn't ready for that just yet, so he clambered down one rung at a time instead.

"Let's go," he said. "I think all three of us need to talk and establish some rules about how this is going to work."

"Rules?"

"Yes, rules," Jonas said firmly. "There are chores around here that still need to get done."

"Chores?" Casey was incredulous. "We have a unicorn in our barn, and you're talking to me about chores?"

Jonas wheeled on her. "Yes Casey. I am. The sun is still coming up and going down ain't it? It's still going up and down on the other side of that gate too. The world isn't stopping for us, and we can't stop for it."

"Dad!"

Jonas put his hand up to forestall any more talking. When they reached the barn, he pointed to the back porch and said, "Find StarFall, and meet me over there."

Casey pounded away and returned a short time later with the steed.

"Okay," he began, "Casey, you translate."

StarFall glanced at Casey in confusion, and she said, "He wants to make rules."

Jonas squinted at his daughter while she folded her arms and speared him with a tight glare of defiance.

"Right then. Assure him…" Jonas began, but, glancing at StarFall, he became momentarily disconcerted over the fact that he was talking with his daughter and a horse. Pretending to gather his thoughts, he huffed and started again. "What I mean to say is that I really want to help get him home. But it's just you and me here, and while I can do plenty of the work, I can't do it all. With me so far?"

"I am," Casey answered, and Jonas could tell by the abrupt monotone in her voice that she already knew where this was going.

"Good. Now I'm willing to give this two full days to get started. After that I expect you to resume all of your chores. And now that you know how important they are, I also want you to be more diligent about practicing with your knives, and that begins today."

"I will," Casey promised quickly.

"And that does not mean you get to neglect your pistols. You have to keep practicing with those too. This is a dangerous place we live in. You have to be ready for the gate, and ready for outlaws and Indians, and wolves and mountain cats, and now we have lizard monsters and who knows what else. Follow?"

Gaze steady, lips set in tight determination, Casey nodded once.

"So you need to be good with both of them. Real good. And you need to prove it to me regularly. If you don't, or you can't, I'm not letting you leave the ranch by yourself, even if you are with him." Jonas tilted his jaw at the unicorn.

Casey exhaled audibly and said, "I understand."

"Right then." Jonas nodded back at her. "That's what I wanted to hear. Now, if it helps, and as long as it means everything needs getting done around here gets done by sundown, I'm willing to let you two make your own schedule."

Casey nodded but remained quiet.

Jonas tilted his head at Casey and said, "I think I'm being pretty fair."

Casey nodded again.

Normally, Jonas would have prompted her to respond, but knowing how disappointed she was, he let it slide. "What does StarFall say?" he asked instead.

Casey translated, then turned back to her father. "He's anxious to begin, but believes you're being fair and has offered to help in any way he can with the chores."

Jonas smiled. "Good." The showdown had gone much better than he had expected. "Good," Jonas repeated. Then he slapped his knees with both hands and stood. "I say we have an early lunch and get right out to the gate and have a look around. Maybe we'll see Taliko, or more likely, he'll find us on the way."

"Really? Today?" Casey finally smiled. "We're going to do this together?"

"Of course," Jonas replied. "We're in this together. I know I can't be much help opening the gate, but I can help you set up a campsite in case you need to take a break, or if it rains."

Casey nodded enthusiastically. "I didn't think of that. Thanks Dad."

After lunch Casey, Jonas, and StarFall struck out for the gate. The trek was uneventful, and they did not pause until they reached Point Lookout and the frolicking brook tumbling under it.

"Explain to StarFall that before they abandoned it, the aril used this tower as a fort. And that Taliko lives under there somewhere. And that he has the lizardlings with him."

"Got it," Casey said, turning away and then back again. "Hold on. What are lizardlings? Are they his children or something?"

Jonas waited before speaking, then replied, "No. I'm not sure what they are and neither is Taliko. He's trying to figure that out. Communicate with them."

"Communicate," Casey echoed.

"Whoa!" she drew up short. "Lizardlings? As in the lizard monsters that attacked us? Those lings?"

Jonas turned toward Casey. "I don't like it either but…it seems very important to Taliko. And we know we can kill them if we have to, if we need to—not that it's easy. But…"

"I can't believe they slipped my mind." Casey shook her head. "Everything is just so tumbleweeds in the wind."

"I know," Jonas said, and the distant fear that he too was overlooking something very important tickled the back of his mind again. "During the war my captain told me that chaos can be a matter of perspective. The man on the front lines is in a storm of bullets and bayonets and often doesn't know if he's winning or losing. His general is farther back; he sees everything and decides which flank to attack and with what company to give them the best chance of winning. Training and discipline ensures that everyone does what needs to be done when it's time to do it."

"What does this have to do with—" Casey started and stopped when her father's look told her he was just coming to that.

"So"—Jonas held Casey's eyes in his own—"it's when things are at their worst that it's most important to stay calm, keep routines in order, and establish what perspective you can. If you can do that, you can make decisions that win the battle."

"Training and routine," Casey said after a moment.

"Exactly."

"So this captain"—Casey sniffed—"he's the real reason I have to keep doing my chores."

Jonas laughed. "Yeah. It's all his fault."

StarFall snorted.

"He all right?" Jonas asked.

Casey spoke with StarFall a moment and then blew out another sigh.

"What is it?" Jonas prompted her again.

"He's frustrated with all our chatter. He wants me to teach him some of our language so he can understand us better and work quicker."

"Why is it he understands your words but not mine?" Jonas asked. "We speak the same language."

Casey queried StarFall, then replied, "He says it's the same reason I was able to see them running through the woods on Friday."

"Your frein?" Jonas guessed.

"My frein." Casey nodded. "I want him to understand me, so my frein puts magic into my words to make sure he does."

"Right," Jonas answered. "I think we went over that last night in the barn. Still, that would be a good idea. And he can learn English? Just to understand me? I suppose he can." Jonas answered his own question while he watched StarFall examine the crumbling outpost. "Or he wouldn't have asked."

"Yeah," Casey mumbled. "Sounds like another chore to me."

"Maybe Taliko can help; they understand each other some too, right?"

Casey brightened. "That's a cherry idea!"

Taliko did not appear while they rested at Point Lookout, but they lingered longer than anticipated because StarFall became very curious about Jonas's harmonica when he witnessed him attempt to call Taliko with it. As a result father and daughter sang several songs for him, after which StarFall told them he had never seen or heard the like, not even among the aril, who are often wondrous singers and musicians.

In time they were moving again, Jonas showing Casey where the stepping-stones were so that her feet remained dry. Then both watched in awe as StarFall vaulted over the fifteen-foot span like he had wings.

"Amazing," Casey breathed.

It was early afternoon when they came to a thick regiment of towering fir trees.

StarFall surged ahead and disappeared straight into the cloying, living wall.

"Whoa!" Jonas gasped, stepping into the tightly interwoven branches where the steed had disappeared and being repelled by them. "How'd he do that?"

"Is this new?" Casey sounded alarmed. "Is the gate behind this somewhere? How do we get in? *Can* we get in?"

"Calm down." Jonas waved his hands in a downward motion. "We have our own way. Your mother showed it to me. The tree maze is a way to keep strangers out, so people don't find the gate by accident."

"Ohh," Casey said with obvious relief. "I thought we might have to go back for axes or something."

"Funny you should say that," Jonas remarked, testing and bending a handful of branches. "Your mother loved all the animals and birds, flowers and trees, just like you always have. Sort of what brought us together." Jonas removed his hat and wiped his brow. "Story for another day. See the hint of copper in some of these pine branches?"

Casey came over for a closer look. "That's beautiful," she said, nodding. "The copper sparkles like little stars when they catch the sun."

"It is," Jonas went on. "These trees are like the pearlwood. From her side. And I almost think if we chopped into this grove that they would somehow know and come through the gate to stop us."

Casey's eyes grew wide. "That's a horrible thought, Dad."

"It could be a last resort for StarFall," he said glumly.

"Well, let's hope it doesn't come to that."

"Let's," Jonas said, rushing back from other dismal thoughts. "And let's see if we can find the way in."

They circled the wide ring several times, and Casey was just beginning to doubt her father knew what he was doing when his hand abruptly vanished through the trees.

"Found it!" Jonas exclaimed and then disappeared into the green wall so swiftly that Casey sucked her next breath through her teeth. When the minutes piled up and he still didn't return, she began to panic.

"Dad! Where are you?" she called, prodding tight branches that were more akin to the seams of a rock wall. "Dad! Come ba—*aaah*!" Casey screeched when his hand popped through and grabbed her.

Then her father's face appeared, and he was laughing so hard she was surprised she hadn't heard him before seeing him.

"That was not funny!" Casey glared at her father.

Jonas laughed harder. Then his face disappeared back beyond the green wall and the sound of his laughter was abruptly cut off. His open hand waited for her, and clasping it tightly, Casey stepped through.

"Nearly impossible to find if you don't know what you're looking for," he said. "Practice going through a few times while I start looking for the entrance to the next ring. We'll mark it somehow when we leave."

Casey watched him go for a moment, unsure about why she needed to practice coming and going. Then decided if finding the second entrance took as long as the first, moving in and out of the ring would help pass the time.

As it was, she got out easy enough but had lots of trouble getting back in. Sometimes she could get a hand through, a foot or even her face, but then the rest of her got stuck.

"Oh, crickets and rotten apples!" she finally shouted at the fir trees. "Let me in!" Thinking speed might be the key, Casey took a few quick steps and slammed into the green wall. All that got her was an aching shoulder and visit to the bed of pine needles under her feet.

"Okay," she said to herself. "Take it slow." Casey moved forward, taking one direct step into the wall and stopping. Then she took a second step and emerged on the other side.

"I did it!" Casey exclaimed. "I did it!"

"There you are! Didn't you hear me calling you?" her father asked, coming around the bend.

Casey looked at him. "Actually, I didn't. I couldn't hear you laughing before either, not until you poked your head out. I think these trees somehow stop sound too."

"Huh," Jonas looked at the wall again with new eyes. "That's an amazing tactical advantage," he noted, plucking a bullet from his gun belt and placing it in the dirt to mark the exit. "At least it would be, if there were a way to hit a target on the other side."

As she watched him, Casey's eyes glowed with youth's exuberant certainty that every mystery had an answer, even sound-buffering pine trees, and that she was on her way to discovering all of them.

In all the pair had to navigate five narrow rings of escalating difficulty to reach the center. Mastering the walk of stepping into the ring and then through was an important key, for sometimes you had to sidestep while in the foliage before stepping forward again; on one occasion they even had to climb.

Her father marked each "slipway" with another bullet. "We should replace these with stones at some point," he remarked while they deciphered the third ring. "Make them less obvious until we know the way by heart. Or maybe just pace them off."

At last they emerged into the hidden half-acre oval that made up the Gategrove.

Inside the afternoon sunlight steaked down through the tall trees at an angle, filling the grove with a flickering, dreamlike atmosphere; slowly, and with measured steps, Casey strode forward from the shadow of the grove wall. The moment she crossed into the dappled light, her skin tingled, though from anticipation or something else, she could not be sure.

"Oh my." Casey stood, gaping at the towering portal and its glistening marble dais.

Jonas looked long on the gateway as well. His thoughts were his own.

The portal arch was fashioned out of granite blocks. Affixed to the center of each facet of every stone was a bright jewel of varying shape, size, and color. Surrounding each jewel was a set of deep, carefully chiseled runes.

The standing stones themselves had been carefully hewn into a perfect rectangular block that was two-feet high, two-feet wide and four-feet deep. The stones were stacked seven high on either side, forming two pillars ten feet apart.

The arch linking them was etched with dark carvings, an unreadable chain of mysterious symbols with no apparent beginning or end. The keystone, looming over twenty feet in the air, was encrusted with an oval desert jasper the size of Jonas's fist, which faced the marble floor.

Casey stepped up on the marble dais, then walked around and under the arch several times, marveling at the runes and gems. "Thank goodness this is hidden," she said. "Anyone finds this and they'll destroy it and sell these stones before the jackrabbit jumps."

Jonas was about to agree with her when Casey noticed StarFall drinking from a small pond at the other end of the hidden clearing and moved briskly toward it.

The water was filled with multicolored fish, scooting and diving with the aid of fanlike fins. A stone fountain stood in the center, carved in the likeness of three graceful swans with turquoise eyes and crisp, clear water pouring gently from their mouths. Their raised wings met in the middle, where they cradled a large flowered basin. Birds sprang between the sculpture and the surrounding trees, chittering and singing happy songs. Facing the pond at each directional point was a smoothed tree stump where two could sit comfortably and gaze upon the pleasantly burbling scene.

"I feel like I remember this place," Casey said distantly. "Not the gate, but this pond. I feel like I've been here before."

"You have been here," Jonas said, coming up behind her. "I used to bring you here when you were little. You'd play at the edge of the water, feeding the fish and birds with bread and grain we brought from home."

Just then, a gray bird shot with red markings that made it look like it was trimmed in flame when it flew landed on Casey's head.

"What in the—" Casey began, but then the bird hopped down to her shoulder and they were eye to eye. "Can you believe this bird?" she laughed. "If you drop on me, there's gonna be trouble," Casey warned her new feathered friend sternly.

The bird cocked its head, chittered back at her a moment, and then flew off.

Jonas laughed. "Just like old times. Maybe he remembers you."

Casey looked at her father. "You think that's possible? Do birds live that long?"

"In here, who's to say what kind of bird that even is?" Jonas answered.

StarFall snuffed and snorted by the gate, gaining their attention.

Casey's eyes widened a few times while the steed communed with her, and Jonas braced himself for what she might say next.

"He says he can't be sure exactly what happened," Casey began. "But the day he got stuck here, some kind of black cloud filled the gate. He crashed into it on his way through. There was an explosion of sorts, and he was knocked out. He doesn't know what it was. Could have been errant magic or something happening on the other side."

"Loose mountain magic," Jonas mused out loud. "Like the lizardlings, I'd wager. Things just keep slipping though."

"Slipping through?" Casey asked. "Like the storms?"

"Like the storms." Jonas nodded. "Sometimes the mountain lets other stuff, nasty stuff, through too. But it's not supposed to happen out here. Mae said it would only happen in the mountain."

More precisely, Jonas added quietly, *in that dashed cave.*

A long moment passed before Casey exclaimed, "What? No. That would be terrible. Don't even think that!"

"What?" Jonas asked, eyes narrow.

"He says gates are usually built by places with loose magic because they draw on it to operate. But in some places, the magic is dangerously erratic. Those gates can shut suddenly, and travelers caught in them are never seen again."

Casey took a deep breath, forcing herself to get the words out. "This isn't supposed to be one of the dangerous places, so it just occurred to him that if the aril opened the gate while he was unconscious and he didn't come back…"

"They think he was killed when the gate closed," Jonas finished for her, shaking his head.

"Which means they're not coming." Casey pursed her lips.

"So it's up to us," Jonas said.

"Me, you mean." Casey sighed.

Seeing his daughter's face, Jonas put more steel into his voice. "We don't know what they're thinking on the other side of that gate. Either way, nothing's changed over here. Nothing's any harder than it already was, is it?"

Casey thought on that for a moment, then her chin rose and her eyes brightened. “No, it isn’t.”

“Right then.” Jonas locked eyes with her and nodded. “Go on and remind him that *we,* have no intention of giving up.”

Casey smiled fiercely and turned away to commune with StarFall.

Jonas looked away before either of them could see his face darken. “For so long nothing,” he muttered to himself. “Why all this now? And where in blazes are you, Taliko?”

Jonas turned suddenly, raising his voice and pointing at his daughter. “Tonight, when we get back. Knives and pistols.”

“Yes, Dad.”

“Both of us,” he grumbled.

He had never told Casey about the cave and did not intend to. It had taken her so long to get over the wolf nightmares, and the Cave of Bones seemed to him something that might start them up again if she knew about it. *Sorry Mae, but if there’s another dead thing it that cave, I’m going to get enough dynamite to bring the whole blasted mountain down on it.*

Casey resumed examining the gate.

“Does he have any idea where to begin or how to open it?” Jonas asked.

Eyes peering into the depths of the sparkling gems, fingers probing the runes, Casey relayed the question to StarFall. “No. Its function is an aril secret. Using gates like this is common where he lives. They get around easily that way. Just like you said. Go through a portal. Get what they need, and come back the same way. So he’s seen them do it lots of times. But they all do it in different ways. Some touch it. Some whisper to it. Some just stand there and it opens for them. They say no one else can learn how do it. Just the aril. But there is no way to know for sure because they’ve never agreed to teach anyone. Like he said last night, that’s why he thinks the law against marrying humans or—what?”

"What?" Jonas raised his eyebrows.

"Humans, or *others*." Casey looked at him.

"Others?" Jonas felt his jaw slip. "So…humans and arils aren't the only people?"

Casey shook her head, eyes glazing over.

Jonas drew his hand over his face and said, "Let's stay focused on opening the gate."

Still speechless, Casey nodded.

"Right then," Jonas said, nodding back and looking up at the top of the arch. "Not much to go on—you get started, and I'll have a better look around outside the maze."

"It'll be getting dark soon," Jonas said at length.

He had returned some time ago and spent the remainder of the afternoon perched on one of the tree stump chairs, staring down into the fish pond, trying and failing to grasp the shadowy sense of fear that was haunting him.

Casey stirred sleepily at the sound of his voice, rubbing her eyes. After walking under and around the portal, touching and examining everything for nearly an hour, StarFall suggested it might be best to simply sit and meditate upon opening the gate. He was right. While she sat there. it felt like half remembered images and memories were brushing up against her thoughts, but each time she tried to focus on one, the idea—or perhaps more accurately, the vision—slipped away.

Casey was certain it was the magic of the gate reacting to her. She just had to learn how to harness and control it. Like breaking in a new stallion.

'Here," her father said, extending his hand. Casey took it and stood, shaking life back into her tingling legs and feet.

"I can feel it, Dad," she told him. "Like it's alive but we don't know how to talk to each other yet."

Jonas flicked his gaze toward StarFall. "I know what you mean."

"You do?"

Jonas nodded. "When I first met your mother, she didn't speak English. But she always seemed to know what I wanted to say and picked it up quick. Along the way she taught me a few of her words too. Mostly for fun, not enough to carry a conversation." Then his eyes took on a faraway look. "Sometimes, though, when we were just sitting, very close and quiet, I felt something. Could almost see flashes, but I couldn't hold them. She told me the fact that I could see anything at all was proof of just how much we cared for each other."

Jonas shrugged. "By that time we knew you were coming and were planning for her to stay, and then…" Jonas shrugged again. "You know the rest."

Disappointed but yet hopeful, the trio exited the Gategrove and headed back to the ranch.

8
THE DOUBLE D DEAL

On Monday, August 10, 1885, Storm Town and its environs were saturated to the roots by a dark, thunder-laden storm that erupted just before sunrise. The storm exhausted itself, and by late morning, the hot sun resumed its scorching vigil with a vengeance. Despite the soggy start—and their travels to and from the Gategrove being plagued by relentless clouds of hornets, honey bees, and other stinging insects—Jonas and Casey set about fulfilling their promise to assist StarFall in getting home with unmitigated homesteader determination.

Hour after hour, day after day, Casey tried to connect with the gate and used breaks to teach the errant unicorn English. Meanwhile, Jonas worked inside the circle and out, cutting branches and fashioning them into a small shelter. Believing it best not to confound his daughter any further with murky possibilities and dismal prospects, Jonas kept quiet, ready to provide what comfort and support was needed if and when it came to it.

For his part Jonas was still grappling with the realization that the arrival of

StarFall had simply been some sort of unicorn misadventure and that the aril still had no intention of returning. It was difficult hiding how he felt about being no closer to ever seeing Mae again, but he had done well keeping it from Casey so far and vowed each morning to carry on.

And so, knowing not how long it would take for Casey and StarFall to resign themselves to failure should it come to that, he buried his personal disappointment and worked diligently to make the grove shelter as sturdy as possible.

He could never have done it so quickly, if at all, without StarFall.

Figuring it was unwise to use any elements of the grove wall to make the shelter, Jonas plied his axes and saws outside on nearby trees. Then, utilizing his innate ability to pass through the barrier unhindered, the steed quickly and easily carried the building materials Jonas crafted outside the ring inside to where they could be assembled, saving Jonas untold time and energy.

A long history of working with regular horses had created habits and expectations that were hard to break, but StarFall's intelligence quickly asserted itself into every task they did together. In fact, it had been StarFall's idea to help him when he saw Jonas struggling to bring his first planks into the clearing. Sure enough, Jonas found he could communicate with StarFall from the outset using hand signals and quickly came to accept the steed as his equal, and in some ways his better.

Late Thursday afternoon, while putting the final nails into the shelter, he mentioned to Casey, "He really trusts us. I'm glad he does. Maybe it's my nature to do different. But given the disposition of the aril and what he must've heard about us humans, I'm surprised how well we're all working together already."

Casey smiled after conferring with StarFall. "He says you knowing about the pearlwood made him feel like he could trust us. And that he could tell from the beginning something was different about me and thinks me being half aril and half human might be a vast improvement on both bloodlines."

Jonas laughed. "Doesn't say much for me."

"Maybe not," Casey giggled with him. "But he also says he talked to the horses in the barn when he first got here and they all like you too. Told him you've always been good to them and they were happy living with us. Said they feel the ranch is a safe place for them."

Jonas had been nailing planks together and paused. "Really?"

StarFall nodded at him.

"Tell him thank you. That means a lot to me."

"Of course, tasty apples might have something to do with it too," Casey added.

"It might, huh?" Jonas laughed. "Speaking of which, I'm going to have to make a run into town tomorrow, trade for supplies. We're getting low on lots of things, and you'll need some stuff for out here too. Why don't you take a break tomorrow? Catch up on your chores or, better yet, come along with me. I don't think it's wise for you to be out here alone."

"I won't be alone. I'll be with StarFall."

Seeing Casey's determination, Jonas nodded, his lips a thin, tight line. "I wish Taliko was around to keep an eye on you. He's been busy with those rotten lizardlings for days."

"We'll be fine, Dad." Casey looked at him squarely. "After all, I'm pretty sure StarFall can outrun anything in the whole canyon."

Jonas glanced over at the hornless unicorn.

"And he fought off three wolves right on our doorstep," Casey reminded him.

Jonas nodded, still looking at StarFall.

"Even killed one of them," Casey added.

"He certainly did," Jonas agreed sullenly, knowing right then and there the matter was settled.

That night their sleep was interrupted numerous times by cracks of cloudless thunder that never brought rain, so Friday, Casey's sixth day working and meditating in the Gategrove, began with a late breakfast.

Finally, after exchanging warm hugs and issuing stern warnings to be careful and lots of severe gesticulating to StarFall to watch over Casey, Jonas set out for Storm Town with an oversized wagonload of apples. Apples that everyone in town was delighted to see.

Arriving from Mountain Road, Jonas paused at the corner of Water Street and Thunderbolt Way to jump on the deck and start tossing out free samples that put a smile on even the sourest face.

By the time he got to the general store, word had spread and there was already a line waiting.

"I haven't seen Jonas in over two weeks!" Jacob Miller was howling at the buzzing mob who had only heard *Tamm Apples are here!* "Whoever got apples didn't get them here."

Just then the bell over the door jingled, announcing the arrival of a new customer, and everyone turned.

"Jonas!" Miller cried happily, even as several others began to applaud.

Jonas froze in his tracks, completely taken by surprise, "Howdy, y'all. Seems to be a commotion; maybe I'll go wet my whistle a bit and come back after."

Jonas turned to go but was affectionately drawn back and pulled to the register with amiable hoots and hollers for him to stay.

The apples were unloaded with happy fervor while Jonas traded for numerous needs including ropes, nails, water skins, pots, blankets, and a cooking kit that he thought would make Casey more comfortable in the shelter, as well as some grain, fresh bread, cheese, beans, salt pork, potatoes, and other vegetables. From the general store he also picked up bullet molds, gun powder, and a new pot in which to melt silver and lead to make more bullets. He was disappointed to discover that Mr. Miller hadn't acquired any new books, but saving the best for last, he cheerfully stopped by the saloon for that beer and traded for some whiskey to enjoy on the porch while watching the sunset.

Hours later he was just tying down the last of his new supplies when a voice called out behind him.

"Mr. Tamm?"

"Yes?" Jonas turned.

During the war, Jonas's regiment had once stumbled onto a stream where he won a bet by being the first to spear a fish. The instant he looked into the piercing blue eyes of the striking woman who had called out to him, he knew how that fish felt.

"Oh, I'm delighted to catch you, Mr. Tamm,"

"I'm sorry, I've traded all my apples already, Misses…"

A mild gust tossed First Street, liberating a shock of raven dark hair from the blue ribbon holding back the woman's tresses; Jonas was forced to wait while she corralled it with a white lace-gloved hand.

"That would be *Miss*—Sherwood," she informed him.

"Right then. Ms. Sherwood." Jonas tipped his hat.

"I'm not here about apples, Mr. Tamm."

Jonas had meant to say, please call me Jonas, but what he said was "You're not?"

"No." She shook her head and eyed him severely. "I'm here about your daughter. Casey I believe it is."

"You believe correctly, Ms. Sherw—"

"I am Storm Town's new teacher, and the rate of Casey's absences this summer has me frightened, Mr. Tamm."

"Frightened?"

"Indeed, sir. Without a proper education, poor Casey's prospects will also be frightening, to say the least." She looked knowingly over his shoulder, and Jonas followed her gaze back to the saloon from which he had just exited. "Don't the prospects for an uneducated young lady, and by that I mean your own daughter, Mr. Tamm, scare you as well?"

"She's passed school age," Jonas turned back to face her. "Turned fourteen in the spring."

"Oh! Fourteen you say," Miss Sherwood said with mock congeniality. "Doesn't that just make all the difference?"

She waited, and eventually Jonas said, "Doesn't it?"

"No, sir, it does not."

"Oh," Jonas said, peering back at the saloon.

"Oh, indeed," Miss Sherwood said with a curt nod. "As August has half flown and I know how much everyone adores those apples of yours, I will trust upon your good judgment to rectify the situation when school resumes after the fall harvest."

"Yes, well, I've been keeping up with—" Jonas began before Ms. Sherwood cut him off a second time.

"When school resumes, for the winter."

Unsure of what to say next, Jonas poked his dusty hat up with his forefinger.

Misreading the gesture, Miss Sherwood tilted her head and smiled with a genuine allure that Jonas could not deny.

"Nice to make your acquaintance Mr. Tamm."

Jonas meant to return the smile but could only frown when she added, "But I do so hate to repeat myself, so I hope we needn't have this conversation again. Good day."

Ms. Sherwood whirled and walked off. When Jonas knew she was safely out of earshot, he mumbled, "It was until you came along."

On the way home with his supplies, Jonas considered Ms. Sherwood, who had certainly gotten both the drop on him and the best of him. Storm Town had a one-room schoolhouse, and as far as he knew, most kids did stop school around fourteen to work full-time. At least they had when he went to school. Casey also seemed to catch on quicker than others her age, probably thanks to her mother. Even so, Jonas routinely made sure to keep up with her learning as best he could and traded for new books for her to read when he could find them. Beyond that, he'd always figured Casey would just inherit the ranch someday. At least if she wanted to. And why not? She loved the orchard, the horses, the animals, and exploring the foothills around Thunder Peak. Which might worry Jonas if Taliko wasn't out there. But he was. And there was also that boy Nash, who never seemed too far away. No doubt the boy was quite fond of Casey, but Jonas had no idea if the feeling was mutual.

So it was that before he had gotten even halfway home, Jonas had decided Casey had lots of good prospects and none of them involved the likes of the Aces High Saloon.

When Jonas did pull the wagon to a halt beside the front porch, it was to the comforting *thunk* of Casey practicing her knives next to the barn. He could also see that many of the timber targets he had left out for her to practice her pistols on were punctured, scared and splintered with new bullet holes.

"How'd it go in town?" she asked when he strode up behind her.

"Good. Most everything we need is in the wagon. You're back early. Where's StarFall?"

"When I focus on the gate too long, I start getting headaches." *Thunk!* Casey hit the target but not a bullseye. "And even though I'm just sitting there, it's exhausting. Like, I-been-haulin'-apples-to-town-on-my-back-for-a-week exhausting."

Jonas nodded and then shook his head from side to side. "I have no ideas about that. What does StarFall think? Where'd you say he was?"

"Not sure really." *Thunk!* "He went for a run, or a walk, or to explore. Maybe he doesn't want to be cooped up. Maybe he's disappointed."

"Disappointed?"

"Yeah." *Thunk!* "Disappointed in me." *Thunk!* "Not having any luck."

"Casey." Jonas held her arm back. "I can't talk to him like you can, but I'm sure he knows how hard this is for you. How"—he chose his next words carefully—"much of a long shot this is to happen right away."

"If at all," Casey muttered, looking down.

"Yes," Jonas said softly, "if at all. But you also just started. I don't recall you being much better than useless with knives or bullets after a week either."

"That's true," Casey cocked a half smile. "And hey." She looked up. "You should be practicing with me. What with the sheriff calling on you more and more, and when I do get that gate open, who knows what the aril will do."

Jonas frowned at a mental picture of aril soldiers leaping through the portal like a swarm of angry sunthorns, then said, "That makes a lot of sense. I think I will. Right now, though, you keep working. I'll get the wagon unloaded and dinner going."

The following morning Jonas accompanied Casey and StarFall back to the grove. To Jonas it seemed there was a diligent silence hovering over them like a storm cloud waiting to burst, and it put him on edge.

Guessing it had something to do with the aura of disappointment Casey described yesterday and not one to wait when something was on his own mind, Jonas struck the frosty quiet inside the Gategrove with unbiased blunt force.

"All right," he said. "We've all got work to do. What is it?"

Casey's expression flashed from morose to blank. "What's what?"

"The silence," Jonas said pointedly. "You two are never this quiet. What's the matter?"

Casey looked at StarFall, then back to her father, and sighed. "Crickets and rotten apples," she barked. "That's just it. I know he's got a bother. I can feel it. But when I ask him about it, he keeps saying it's the bees."

"The bees? Aren't they just aggravated we keep passing by?"

"No," Casey replied. "He says they shouldn't be stinging him. Not here, not anywhere. Some kind of unicorn magic. And maybe that's true because all the times I've explored, I've never been stung either. But I think there's more. He doesn't want to say, but I can feel it, Dad. There's something else."

StarFall whinnied loudly.

"The wolves that chased him down?" Jonas asked, his face tightening. *Seven bells, Taliko! Where are you? You should be here helping us with this.*

"Okay, maybe." Casey acquiesced. "But it's not just the wolves and the bees—are you listening to me, Dad?"

"I am," Jonas said, pointing at StarFall and walking toward him. "Not just the wolves and the bees. Is he bleeding?"

StarFall turned away as Jonas neared.

"Hey now!" Jonas said sternly, patting him on the neck.

"What do you mean 'bleeding'?" Casey rushed after her father. "Where?"

"We're all friends here," Jonas continued softly. "At least I think we are. Let's have a look."

But each time they tried to face him, StarFall shook his snowy mane and craned his head up in the opposite direction, blocking their view of his forehead.

Finally, Jonas locked eyes with him and said, "Casey, remind him we're all helping each other. That he can trust us. He doesn't need our word. He spoke to our horses."

StarFall finally snorted in resignation. "I know," the unicorn sighed in Casey's mind, lowering his head as she repeated it for her father. "But time runs short for me."

"What does that mean?" Jonas asked.

StarFall whinnied softly in despair. "This Crossing was supposed to herald my first Wrivening."

"Riv…riv-en-ning?" Casey stumbled over the unfamiliar word.

StarFall nodded, and another blood trail seeped from a fold in his forehead and ran down toward his nose.

The moment she saw it, Casey winced at the pain she imagined he must be feeling. "You mentioned that before," she said gently. "Wrivening. But I don't know what it means."

StarFall lowered his head, then picked it up again, eyes filled with resolve. "The hour of my first Wrivening, my first horn, draws near. If I do not get home soon for the ceremony, it will not grow. I will lose it, and any magic that comes with it. Forever."

"Lose it forever? Well, that's just awful." Casey stamped her foot. "StarFall! I thought the ice apples were fixing everything. Why didn't you tell me about this? I could work longer, try harder."

"Stop." StarFall peered at her. "I had hoped this would work quickly. If it had, it would remain something you never needed to know. With all you do you hardly sleep. To that there is the hidden work your sire does. Both of you are already doing all you can, and I did not wish to add to the burden."

Casey glanced at her father and then back to StarFall. "What work is my father doing? This hidden work?"

"The shelter in the grove fits both of us. His recent modifications to the horse home make it easier for me to come and go. His efforts prepare for failure. His efforts welcome me for a lengthy stay. Perhaps a permanent one."

Casey glared at her father. Jonas kicked at the ground but said nothing.

"Fine." Casey turned back to StarFall. "But is there anything else *I* can do. What kind of ceremony is it? Can't we do it here?"

"Perhaps." StarFall gazed in the distance. "But it requires the assistance of a maiden unicorn."

Jonas lifted his eyebrows when Casey translated that bit, but said nothing.

"Oh," Casey replied. "And our horses can't help? Maybe even a little?"

StarFall shook his head. "They are males, and they are not unicorns. The ceremony involves licking my forehead to soften the bone and prepare an aperture for my first horn to grow through. Maiden unicorns use their frein to accomplish this. Perhaps if there was an Earther filly in the barn, it would give me extra time, but such a remedy is untried so I do not know."

When Casey finished the explanation, Jonas nodded and said, "I think a new filly was born over at the Double D some few seasons ago. I'll ride out, bring a few apples, make some small talk, and see if…see if we can reach an agreement." Jonas rubbed his chin thoughtfully. "Pretty certain she has enough hands on the ranch, but I can always lend her Cotton or Cross to keep the work going if it comes to that."

StarFall nodded after Casey told him the plan to lend a horse from their stable to bring a maiden into theirs. "The effort would be welcome. The Wrivening, it is not without pain. That is why I have been avoiding you, to hide my discomfort while you work. There are times it is nearly unbearable, and I don't want to distract you."

Casey patted his neck, feeling awful about thinking StarFall was mad at her.

Jonas rested a hand on Casey's shoulder and squeezed softly. "I'm sorry. I didn't want to talk about the possibility of this not working. Of you—"

"And we're not going to talk about it," Casey said. "This is going to work. The widow's filly is going to give us the extra time we need, and it's all going to work out. I know it."

Jonas nodded and placed a gentle hand under her chin. "I'm proud of you. And you know what? Your mom will be too when StarFall gets home and she hears all about how her daughter helped him get back."

The moment he said it, Jonas felt a cold hand clasp his heart, but before he could understand why, Casey hugged him and said, "Thanks, Dad. Now get going. StarFall's offered to carry you back."

"Carry *me*?" Jonas cocked his head. "Us, you mean. You can't stay here alone."

"C'mon, Dad." Casey rolled her eyes and then said to StarFall, "You're on his side?"

"Casey—" Jonas began.

"No." Casey thrust her arms out. "I'm staying. Even if it's just a couple hours. I'll be safe. I know the woods like the back of my hand. And I'm the one who led us to Arrowhead Pond, remember? I'll head back when the sun is highest. I promise. You have to let me do this. Please, Dad. You have to."

Casey folded her arms and looked off toward the arch, lower lip trembling.

Jonas grit his teeth and breathed deep, ready to order his daughter to leave with them and steeling himself for the fight. Then he saw her shoulder sash filled with Mae's throwing knives, and the words died in his throat. Saw the long knife belted around her hips, and amidst admitting to himself that he wished her Navy was holstered there as well, remembered how how he had gone to war when he wasn't much older than she was now.

"All right." He relented. "Because this is urgent."

Casey looked at him and nodded, smiling tightly against the fear he might suddenly change his mind.

"All right," her father said again. "Till top sun. Then heading home, knife in hand."

"Top sun," Casey repeated. "Knife in hand."

"Right then," Jonas said, turning his eyes on StarFall. "He's really agreed to carry me?"

"He has," Casey said.

"That's a big deal, I think. Especially if he's in pain. Tell him I'd be honored, and will never, ever tell anyone."

StarFall reared up suddenly, and Casey's eyes brightened. "You made him laugh!"

Jonas smiled and said, "Tell him to move next to that bench."

Casey turned away and back with a nod while StarFall moved into position.

Jonas took a deep breath and winked at her. Then, before allowing himself to think any better of it, the woodsman promptly sprung up on the seat and used it to vault onto the steed's back without a stirrup.

"Top sun," he said one last time.

"Knife in hand." Casey waved him off. "I promise."

Seeing her sit on the marble dais in front of the gate, her expression full of renewed determination, Jonas felt his heart swell with pride.

Then he sensed the grove wall closing in on him and turned—the tightly woven branches were just feet away.

"Wait! Is this gonna hurt?"

StarFall kept going.

Jonas closed his eyes, and they disappeared into the trees.

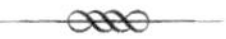

Passage through the grove wall was a blur. It reminded Jonas of trying to open his eyes under the frothy water of a stirred-up watering hole, and he could only wonder at the magic that allowed StarFall to move unhindered through the tangled limbs with him on his back.

They cleared the maze barrier, and the abrupt burst of the equine engine below him, greeting the open space, reminded Jonas of a cavalry charge.

Afterward he would swear that through every graceful turn and during every leap over every bramble and boulder, especially the ones during which he had to close his eyes, he could hear the bugles of the past urging them all the way home.

They made it back to the ranch in under thirty minutes. Given the tangle of the woods, it was a feat Jonas would have thought impossible. But there they were.

StarFall came to halt, and Jonas jumped down. As fast and exciting as the trip was, Jonas was no bareback rider, and found himself thankful to be back on his own feet.

Remembering what Casey had said about learning their language, Jonas gestured around with both hands and said, "Home."

StarFall pawed the ground. Jonas said, "Barn" and pointed at it, and StarFall pawed the ground again.

Jonas smiled at the hornless unicorn. "I'm trying. I had a lot of one-sided conversations around here until Mae and Casey came along. It's only been a week; knowing that you're really listening takes some getting used to."

Jonas patted StarFall's neck and then saddled up Rebel.

When he had finished, he pointed at StarFall and said, "You." Then he pointed at the ground. "Home. We don't need Widow Dorn asking questions and telling folks about a magnificent black colt at the Tamm Ranch and Orchard."

Jonas tried to ride out but was forced to pull up when StarFall followed him.

Raising his hands in what he hoped was a stopping motion, he tried to communicate his wishes a second time with words and hand gestures. "StarFall, wait here. StarFall, home. Jonas, go."

StarFall looked at him blankly, and Jonas got another idea. Tightly pulling on Rebel's reins, he shouted, "Whoa! Rebel, whoa!"

Jonas gestured back and forth to StarFall and Rebel several times until StarFall stepped closer and whinnied at Rebel. Rebel whinnied and snorted a reply.

StarFall backed up, and Jonas said, "StarFall, wait. StarFall, whoa!"

The stallion looked Jonas in the eye a moment and then glumly turned and headed back for the barn.

"Right then." Jonas exhaled, and turning Rebel about with a tight tug on the reins, he galloped off down the road. "Let's get you a dancing partner."

Along the way he considered what he knew about Widow Connie Dorn.

Growing up she was never considered beautiful; her manner was too disciplined to allow for grace and her features simply too rugged. However, at leisure she surprised many with a sudden, easy smile and a boisterous laugh that could fill a room. All told that made her a perfect match for her eventual husband.

David Dorn Jr. had inherited the Double D Ranch from his father, and from the moment God set him upon the earth, he showed little of the physical or mental diligence required to run a ranch on his own. Once he was of age, he spent most of his nights drinking and carousing in Storm Town. Then routinely rose late to join his father and the hands in the fields or tending the cattle and slept walk through most of the day, rarely doing anything productive unless explicitly directed to accomplish a task.

When his parents were both gone and it fell upon David's shoulders to run the place, the ranch lost money until it sat on the verge of bankruptcy.

There was just no telling how Connie saw through his raggedy figure and fading prospects. Perhaps she liked a challenge. Perhaps there were no other gentleman callers. Either way, the warm, open affection they shared during their wedding vows was as undeniable as the imminent disaster that seemed to be the financial future of their union.

Everyone had been invited to the Aces High after the wedding, and even Jonas, in the guise of the seldom-seen good neighbor, showed up and raised a mug to Storm Town's newest couple. As then, there were still very few marriages in the shadow of Thunder Peak, so each one was a major event that drew all the residents from their daily routines. In Storm Town nearly everyone preferred their solitude, so many of them were faces that hadn't been seen in months.

Later it was hard to say exactly how or when it happened, but David appeared less and less at the saloon. Each time he did show up in town, he looked leaner and cleaner. Those who rode out to the property remarked how fences were being mended, the barn repaired, shrubs cleared, and crops grown and tended like in the old days. Mayhap even better than the old days. So it was that the Double D was back and better than before, with Connie making the financial decisions and David running the ranch hands.

It was a wonderful six years for Connie and David, right up until his death of tuberculosis.

After that it was easy to see the pain in Widow Dorn's eyes, and years later it lingered still. But the business never faltered, she made sure of that, and even now the Double D was still one of the more prosperous ranches in Itza Chu Canyon.

That was all Jonas knew of Widow Dorn. They were good neighbors, and they had a long-standing pact she never shied from. Specifically, taking Casey in for a night or two when Jonas was deputized. For that he couldn't be more thankful, and he had told her on many occasions that he was in her debt, a marker she could cash in whenever she saw fit, for whatever was in his power to give.

Such was on his mind as Jonas tied Rebel to a hitching post out front of the homestead and walked up to the house, ready to bequeath her another marker.

He knocked on the door and then turned back to look at the grounds. Everything appeared maintained and well-tended. Connie always loved the animals, especially horses. Maybe that was the way to approach this.

The door opened behind him. "My, my," a lady's voice sang out cheerfully, and when Jonas turned and saw Alice Sherwood standing with her hands at her narrow waist, he fell back a step.

"Aunt Connie!" she called back into the house. "A genuine Thunder Peak mystery has blown our fine neighbor Mr. Jonas Tamm all the way to our doorstep."

Alice's gaze swung back to find his, and Jonas resisted the urge to step back a second time.

"We do so rarely see you in these parts, that one can only wonder if it be a gust of good fortune or an ill wind blowing."

Still captured by her striking blue eyes, Jonas asked, "Ms. Sherwood, are you quite certain that you're a schoolteacher?"

Ms. Sherwood tilted her head, and he informed her, "Because the way you keep getting the drop on me, I'm quite certain you must be an outlaw."

Ms. Sherwood's lips smiled first, then her face broke into what Jonas considered to be a delightful smile and she laughed pleasantly.

"So," she said, "there is some charm hiding behind that carelessly handsome wall. Be forewarned, Mr. Tamm, I still expect to see young Casey in class after the harvest."

"I am forewarned," Jonas said with a slight bow. "Now, as it turns out, I have arrived with an offer, perhaps even a deal for the Widow Dorn, if she is about the premises to discuss business."

Ms. Sherwood stepped aside and gestured beyond the doorway. "By all means, please do come in."

Through the doorway was a well-appointed sitting room where the Widow Dorn rose from a sturdy rocking chair. "Ah, Jonas. Welcome. Good to see you. Have you met my niece Alice?"

"I have," Jonas said, crossing over to take her hand. "And good to see you too, Connie. The ranch looks to be doing well."

"Quite well," she replied with a hint of sadness in her eyes. "Been lucky with a few new hands." Connie retook her seat and waved toward a chair for Jonas to do the same. "They keep their eyes on the road, like everyone else who comes to Storm Town, but you know well as I it's the ones who are tired of running and brave enough to hide in plain sight that make the best help around here. Still, they haven't tried to cheat me, and they work hard. Or maybe they're just afraid of all the ghost stories I tell them about what happens to thieves that try to take from the Peak. Either way, the Double D rolls on."

Jonas nodded as he sat down. "Thunder Peak's spirit of vengeance does well by us all," he said, and the three of them chuckled.

"Now," Connie said, "what brings you here?"

Jonas looked at Connie and got straight to the point. "Took possession of a new colt. Striking. Strong. Fast. Black like a starless sky, but he's got a mane like moonlight. I heard you might have a new filly, and I was hoping we could pair them up. See what happens."

Connie nodded her head, and Jonas saw that she began rocking a little more swiftly than before. "Interesting," she said. "What's in it for me?"

Jonas didn't have the time and never had the inclination to bargain, so he went right to his best offer. "Anything that comes of it, you can buy me out at forty percent."

"Sixty-forty?" Connie asked.

"Yes, ma'am." Jonas nodded. "Or, I'll pay you top dollar at seventy percent to keep him myself."

"Seventy!" Connie repeated, eyes sparking. "Quite generous of you."

Jonas inclined his head. "Well, I am in your debt for when you take Casey in, so there's that."

The Widow Dorn stopped rocking. "And?"

Jonas smiled to acknowledge her acumen. "And," he continued, "the colt's only here a short spell. He's on his way to my family's spread back in Texas. So, to make this work, I need to bring your filly to my barn. Today. When I leave."

From past experience Jonas knew that when Connie rocked in her chair, it was a good sign. When she didn't, it wasn't.

"Interesting," Connie said again.

The chair remained motionless, and Jonas frowned inwardly. His offer was more than fair. The horse hadn't been seen in this canyon that was worth seventy percent. Connie should have been jumping at it. But she wasn't, and he didn't know why.

Jonas rarely, if ever, attempted to drive a hard bargain. Truth was, he didn't know how. Most everyone agreed that Jonas could be getting much more for his apples than he did. That was fine with him. He preferred to be regarded as a fair negotiator, not a stingy one. He believed that was part of the reason everyone kept coming back for his apples. He was not motivated by money or gold. Nor could he eat all those apples. He wanted to be comfortable, and left alone, which was why Storm Town suited him. As a result, if Widow Dorn had motives Jonas was unaware of, the shrewd businesswoman most certainly had the upper hand.

"So," Connie said, breaking the silence at last, "you have a young, fast colt who needs a friend. If anything results of it, I can keep it for sixty-forty, or sell it to you for seventy-thirty. And that's it?"

Jonas peered at her a moment and then spread his hands. "What else is there?"

"How about part of the stake?" Connie said flatly.

"Stake? What stake?"

Connie smiled thinly and looked knowingly at him. "Please, Jonas. We are friends here. Let's speak plainly and honestly."

"That's all I know how to do, Connie. We've been good neighbors for quite a while now. You know that."

Still smiling sweetly, still looking at Jonas, Connie asked her niece, "Do you believe him, Alice?"

Alice started slightly at being drawn into the conversation. Recovering quickly, she looked at Jonas while sipping her tea. The silence lingered, broken only by the gentle clink of her cup settling back in its saucer.

Alice put cup and saucer on the table, then sat back and folded her hands, all with her eyes still on Jonas.

Despite being a veteran of the Civil War and more gun fights than he could remember, Jonas felt the heat rising in his face and sweat breaking out on his back.

"I do," Alice replied at last, and Jonas thought he detected the faintest of smiles.

"Well, then," Connie said, "the next man lies to Alice without her knowing it will be the first, so I shall believe you."

"Excellent," Jonas said. "Then we have a deal."

"Not just yet." Connie tilted her head.

Ahh, Connie. Jonas sighed silently. *I know you saved Dave from the bottom of a whiskey bottle, but sometimes I wonder if you didn't kill him anyway.*

"Right then," Jonas said out loud. "Speak your mind. How do we make this happen?"

"The Full Moon Ride."

Jonas looked from Connie to Alice and back again. "Full Moon Ride?"

Connie smiled, and her eyes danced with a light unseen seen since her wedding day.

"It's an endurance race they're setting up from Storm Town to the stagecoach station at Itza Chu Landing and back."

"The Landing?" Jonas felt his jaw drop. "All anyone's going to get racing down the shaft to that scorpion-infested hoodoo is a lame horse and a broken neck."

"Maybe so," Connie agreed. "But for those an event like this attracts, the danger's part of the fun. That and the money."

Jonas nodded. "The stake you were alluding too."

"Quite right," Connie said, eyes burning fiercely. "I hear the whole thing started at Sticky Jack's."

Jonas rolled his eyes. Storm Town had two saloons. The Aces High had a bar, a stage, and a piano, while Sticky Jack's had a bar, a piano, and gambling. Over the many years he'd lived beside Thunder Peak, Jonas could count on one hand the times he'd been to Sticky Jack's.

"Couple of ranchers playing pharaoh, bragging and drinking their way to a fifty-dollar bet on their horses," Connie continued. "Supposedly four more, including the dealer, wanted in on it. Fools keep drinking. Race gets longer. Stakes go up to a hundred, and before long, a total of six gamblers shook hands on it."

"That's outside the valley. Seventy or eighty miles of hard riding." Jonas shook his head. "But for five hundred bucks, I guess it's worth it."

"You'd think so," Connie said, nodding, "but sadly, the whole thing was going to fall through. Apparently, soon as the next day, all parties concerned were laughing it off, calling it liquor talk and ready to pretend it never happened."

At that precise moment, Connie's chair began to rock.

What did you do, Connie? Jonas wondered.

"Best I figure, word got out somehow, snaked its way to Tombstone."

"Tombstone?" Jonas's eyes bulged.

"Indeed." Connie smiled.

Jonas, already sensing he would be deputized over this lunacy, slumped back in his chair and began to rub his temples. "Last thing we need here in our quiet corner of the world is people drifting over from the likes of Tombstone."

Connie, however, was positively alight with excitement over the prospect. "The race is up to seventeen now. Seventeen, Jonas! And probably more still thinking about it."

Jonas exhaled audibly. "Lot of money for the winner." Then added to himself: *Lot of trouble for Storm Town. How'd you let this happen, Tanner?*

"It certainly is." Connie smiled like Ace Holis dropping four aces on the table—as the saying went in Storm Town—and Jonas braced himself. "But is it enough to make you enter that new colt in your barn?"

Jonas clenched his teeth. "Enough to make me wish I could enter the new colt in my barn." *Meanwhile here I am bargaining away his children like he was some common stallion—and for something that might not even work. Still, it's the only chance he's got, so what choice do I have? Either way, probably best not tell StarFall or Casey about this...agreement I'm making on his behalf.* Jonas flicked his eyes toward Connie, who obviously believed he was considering the race. Taking a deep breath, he tried to sound more conflicted than he really was. After all, he still needed to take that filly with him when he left.

"This race draws everyone you think it will, Sheriff Tanner will be looking to deputize me," he said at last. "Plus this colt is on a layover, waiting for my brothers to send someone to pick him up. They won't be happy if he's lame when they get here. Beyond that, I've no mind whether he's truly up to an endurance race from Storm Town to Itza Chu Landing and back. Still, if anything changes, I'll bring you in. Twenty percent of any winnings seem fair to you?"

Connie didn't even try to hide her disappointment.

Alice, however, seemed pleased and said as much, "A sound decision on all accounts, Mr. Tamm."

Connie threw her niece a look that all but said, *Whose side are you on?*

Jonas inclined his head. "Thank you, and it is long past time you call me Jonas, Ms. Sherwood."

Ms. Sherwood smiled, dipped her chin, and blinked slowly.

Jonas felt the tension leave the room. Then Ms. Sherwood added, "I should also think, Jonas, that you are quite concerned for Casey, who is already without her natural parents and in your charge, though you have yet to voice as much."

Jonas sat back and looked at Connie. He hadn't forgotten. It just seemed inappropriate to him to bring her up, but now that Alice had, he was happy to let the schoolteacher help him drive this bargain home.

"Quite the contrary, Ms. Sherwood. I've known your aunt for quite a while. Because of our arrangement for when the sheriff deputizes me, an arrangement I would never jeopardize, Connie knows Casey is my primary concern in all dealings without my having to say so. Isn't that right, Connie?"

Connie's rocking had slowed to nearly a stop, but she smiled fondly at the mention of Casey. "This everyone here at the Double D knows to be true. She's welcome here any time. In fact, please send her around, or bring her yourself, for tea, sometime soon. I miss that girl like she were my own."

Jonas thought that was a good time to stand and did so, crossing over to take her hand. "I will, Connie. I promise. And thank you."

They exited the house, and Connie quickly summoned a ranch hand to bring Jonas the filly he had been bargaining over.

"Won't need that." Jonas waved away the saddle tack when the hand returned. "Just a bridle."

While the ranch hand placed the headgear on, Jonas asked him, "She have a name?"

"Bonnie," the man answered, glancing at him.

"Bonnie?"

The cattleman nodded. "After blue bonnet. Widow Dorn's favorite flower."

"I see," Jonas replied, taking the reins and noticing for the first time the many blue bonnets blooming around the ranch. "Thanks."

"I hear that Ms. Sherwood likes them as well, in case you were wondering."

Jonas looked at the vaquero again and tipped his hat. "Thanks again; good to know."

The man winked and gave him a knowing nod.

Right then. Jonas looked away. *I'm glad this is over.*

"C'mon, Rebel," Jonas barked, simultaneously nudging his feet and tugging on Bonnie's lead.

The horse behind him stumbled, and looking back hurriedly, Jonas was relieved to see that she was fine. Wouldn't do to turn her ankle before they even got on the road.

Then he glanced over at the porch and saw Connie smiling broadly as she spoke with Alice. Turning back toward the trail quickly so they wouldn't catch him watching, Jonas wondered briefly at what it could mean.

Very briefly. Connie was just too darn crafty for him, and knowing he had more immediate concerns, Jonas pushed the whole negotiation from his mind. He had accomplished what he had set out to do, and that was the most important thing right now. Hopefully there would be time enough to worry about any coincidental affairs that resulted if and when they arose.

The way between the Double D and the Tamm Ranch and Orchard was primarily flat, but as Jonas's stretch was the last piece of cultivated land before the Chiricahua Mountains, the tree stands got thicker along the way until one crested a small hill that looked down upon the last open space before the Thunder Peak foothills and the forbidding mountain range beyond.

As Jonas galloped closer, he saw StarFall emerge from the barn. The colt pawed the ground impatiently while he removed the bridle from Bonnie.

Once that was done, StarFall cantered up quickly and seemed to communicate his needs to the filly. Bonnie then began to vigorously lick his forehead, where his budding horn was trapped beneath skin and bone.

StarFall shuddered mightily after a time, and Jonas got the impression that the plan was working. To what degree he could not be certain, but the more StarFall relaxed, the more he surmised things moved toward a positive outcome.

Quite suddenly StarFall looked at Jonas and pawed the ground, an action the rancher took to indicate the steed's thanks, but before Jonas could say anything, the stallion glanced out at the road and swiftly wheeled off for the barn. Bonnie followed him.

Turning about, Jonas saw Casey's friends Nash and Savannah coming down the trail and sighed. Wouldn't do having them follow him into the barn, where they could get a good look at StarFall, so squatting, he began probing Rebel's legs and hooves for bruises, burs, and stones.

"Mornin', Mr. Tamm." Nash greeted him as the pair strode up.

Jonas stood and flashed a smile. "Howdy, Nash. Ms. Winston." Jonas doffed his hat and performed an exaggerated bow that made Savannah giggle. "You two looking for Casey?" he asked, resetting his hat.

"Yes, sir," answered Nash. "Haven't seen her about all week."

"Or school neither," Savannah added.

"Casey be done with schoolin'. I told you." Nash waved his hand at her.

"That's not what Ms. Sherwood said," Savannah shot right back.

"Okay." Jonas raised his hands to quiet them. "The particulars are we cooled our heels too often this summer and now we're going sunup to sundown to catch it up. That means Casey's about her own chores every day and I'm not fixing for her to get distracted; lots of work still needs doing in the orchard, work that's going to tie us up another week." Jonas looked at them a moment, then added, "At least."

"Ms. Sherwood's not going to be happy to hear that," Savannah warned.

Jonas rolled his eyes toward the sky and then back to Savannah. "Of that I'm certain. But I've spoken to Ms. Sherwood, quite recently in fact, and we've come to an understanding. Casey may yet head back for a little more school after the harvest season."

"Really?" Savannah clapped and stuck her tongue out at Nash. "Told you!"

"But not this week," Jonas added quickly. "Now, I've got chores myself that need doing, so move on out, and take your trouble with ya," he added with a squint that made Savannah squirm back with a happy screech. "And don't worry—I'll let Casey know you come by and tell her to round you up soon for a splash in the pond."

Looking quite glum, Nash said, "Thank you, Mr. Tamm." Then brother and sister turned about and headed back up the trail.

Jonas shook his head, blew out his lungs, and led Rebel to the barn to get unsaddled. Realizing he might as well get all the animals fed, Jonas quickened his step. Casey was alone in the Gategrove, and he hoped to meet her on the way back if not rejoin her by noon.

9
CLASH OF SABERS

Time passed.

Casey had no idea how much time. It seemed like minutes and it seemed like ages since her father and StarFall had departed.

Since then she had begun to see things. Feel things. Hear things.

There were lush forests full of vibrant trees, bright with multicolored leaves and birds, clear blue streams and lakes rife with fish, and deeper down, hidden in the dark, massive creatures that seemed to stir when she looked in on them. In the distance a vibrant plateau glimmered with the pink and purple hues of dusk. Tucked in among the trees and hills, a great city of sculpted marble and granite beckoned. In the center of the city was a square with many flags of mysterious design snapping in the breeze.

And there! On a dais of blue-tinted stone was an arch just like the one before her.

The visions were exhilarating. Full of strange, mystical sensations she could not describe.

Casey opened her eyes and gasped: several of the arch stones were glowing! She had done it! She had connected with the gate!

Without warning, a sand-colored eldritch spark burst from the keystone's desert jasper. Snapping like a whip, it connected with a ruby on the left side of the arch. Then a red bolt snapped and hissed across to a topaz stone, which in turn hurled a crackling yellow tendril to an emerald directly opposite.

Before long the energy streams were crackling back and forth too swiftly for Casey's eyes to follow, forming an intricate web inside the portal. With each zap and sizzle of a new strand, the view of the square with its snapping pennants grew clearer. One flag was bigger than the others, and she could clearly see its crossed golden feathers flying in the sky.

Then a hooded figure frantically waving some kind of wooden staff came into view. He was saying something. Casey couldn't make it out at first; then a few more strands connected and the words became clearer. "Ut ar thon?" or some such. Whatever it meant, the figure repeated it over and over.

Casey opened her mouth to respond, to let them know she was here, to say that StarFall was okay, that he needed to get home and that they should come get him when billowing, black smoke began seeping into the gateway from below. Filling the portal, obscuring her vision.

Casey sat confused for a moment. Because of the flickering energy filling the arch, the view was like a puzzle with missing pieces. Constantly changing and fading in and out. Sometimes she could see things in it, and sometimes she saw through them. Therefore, she could not be sure if the darkness was part of the vision in the gate or on the dais with her.

Gritting her teeth, Casey focused on the gate until she could almost see the hooded figure's face. It too looked confused and apprehensive.

"What is that?" She pointed. "Is that supposed to happen?"

The figure turned around. *He can see me!* Casey realized suddenly. *Maybe even hear me! But he's looking back over his shoulder, so he doesn't see the smoke. And that can only mean…*

The pulsing black mass expanded to the size of the arch. Looking up at it, Casey felt suddenly small, as if she was about to be swallowed up by a black pit.

Heart racing, she focused instead on the hooded figure in the portal. His staff was glowing now, and it looked like he was shouting.

Oh no, the dark knife of dismay plunged into her heart. *StarFall said a black cloud stopped him from going home. This must be it!*

"Stop!" Casey found her voice again. "StarFall is here! We're friends! I'm just trying to help him get home! But there's black smoke in the gate, and it doesn't work!"

The figure stopped moving and cocked his head curiously.

Then angry red eyes snapped open in the smoke. Drawn by her shouts, they swung down and fixed their searing glare on Casey, forcing her into timid silence.

Still coiling and curling, the smoke swiftly rolled up on itself until it hovered in the center of the gate.

The burning eyes blinked away, but still caught in their paralyzing spell, Casey remained quiet and motionless, watching the smoke study the tendrils of web lightning and then surge into them, causing a dreadful, screeching flash.

Slammed by a disorienting roar of pain in her head, Casey winced and looked away,

Several long seconds passed before the screaming in her skull died off, but Casey was only allowed a handful of gasps before she was seized again by agony. This one a searing sliver in her bosom that left her writhing back and forth on the dais like someone, or something, was ripping her soul from her chest.

"Help," she called weakly. "Someone, please; help me."

Above her the menacing black cloud still hovered in the gate, churning in the sparkling eldritch filaments. Then she heard it. Beyond the burning in her chest, in the back of her mind where the screaming had been—a howl of pure joy.

Finally, with a blinding, sizzling flare that forced Casey to roll away from the heat, the mystical energy curtain belched a tremendous crack, like the sound of two huge rocks colliding, and disappeared.

Panting heavily on her hands and knees, Casey opened her eyes to find the eerily quiet black cloud looming over her.

With a swift curl of smoke, the eyes returned, burning red and malevolent, examining her. Eyes like the ones in her nightmares. Eyes that filled her bones with icy dread.

A wolf's eyes.

The cloud was never loose magic.

It's alive!

I have to get up.

Get up!

Casey tried to stand, to swallow her fear and defend herself with her knives, but a great weakness assailed her entire body, and unable to keep her eyes open, she toppled over wearily and lay motionless on the dais.

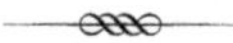

Taliko sat by the creek upstream from Point Lookout, studying the lizardlings frolicking around the water's edge. Ruefully, he realized that several days had slipped by while he held them underground trying to establish basic communication. In that, at least, he had been successful. Finally, he had allowed them back outside, eager to test a theory but fearful of what he might learn.

Reaching down, he gently scooped up a turtle and showed it to the one he called Paal. He had chosen Paal because he seemed of higher intelligence and the most receptive to him. He was fairly certain the one he called Zil was their actual leader, but so far that one continued his belligerence and remained resistant to his overtures of kindness and friendship. If that did not change soon, something would have to be done about him for the sake of the group. Something permanent that would assure the divided hearts and minds of the group aligned with Paal and not Zil.

Taliko showed the turtle to Paal and pointed at himself and the turtle several times, trying to pass on the idea that his Maker had evolved him from the reptile in his hands.

Paal watched for several moments. Then his eyes lit up and he dashed off, indicating for two others to join him as they sprinted into the woods.

Taliko watched them go, smiling appreciatively at Paal's natural knack for command. Then his eyes fell upon Zil, staring after them as well, teeth bared in resentment.

Yes, something would have to be done about that one soon.

Paal and his comrades returned a short time later. Standing before Taliko, Paal opened his hands to reveal a small, red-skinned lizard with long yellow stripes and a blue face that abruptly scurried up and around his arm.

Reaching out and taking the lizard in his scaled claw, Taliko pointed at the lizard and Paal with a questioning grunt.

Paal and the others stood taller, thumping their chests and nodding vigorously.

Taliko smiled through his misgivings and held the creature up to examine it more closely. The resemblance between the two could not be denied.

So, the origin of the lizardlings does not lie within the Cave of Bones. It is similar to my own but dark in nature.

Hopefully that does not make them beyond help.

Is this another attempt to destroy Casey? Or one to perish StarFall? Perhaps both? More importantly, were they sent through the gate? Or is their Maker here?

So many questions…

A distant crack heralded the unmistakable sent of an eldritch flare in the air.

Taliko tensed. *That came from the Gategrove!*

Casey had been working with the gate all week, trying to open it. Had something gone wrong, or was something coming through?

Taliko focused immediately on the task at hand: the lizardlings. It was obvious that they too sensed the magical disturbance. Most of them had scurried fearfully into hiding spots around the cave leading under Point Lookout, while others had joined Zil, looking expectantly into the woods.

With a guttural command, he gathered them all before the cave, attempting to balance control with calm and get them out of the magically charged air and into the safety of the burrow. But just as the lizardlings were ready to march down into the dark, another energy flux, this one glazed with evil, shattered the calm. Amid this new round of chaos, the lizardlings began snapping and clawing at each other, returning to madness.

The same madness he had seen during the attack.

The Lizardling Maker. It has to be!

Taliko growled silently. For better or worse, there was no more time, the reckoning for the lizardlings had come, and he had to act swiftly.

Grabbing his bo-staff from where it rested at the front of the cave, he struck the wall with its silver top, causing a shower of sparks that quieted the lizardlings.

Zil and three others bared their teeth at him in defiance.

Wasting no time, Taliko clubbed the henchmen senseless with three swift strikes. Then he marched on Zil and forced him down onto his back in deference and stood there for a long moment with the silver tip of his staff pointed at the reptilian's chest.

Better to destroy him now, Taliko thought, but his heart ached at the thought, and he simply could not do it.

Instead Taliko clacked his fangs, a warning to any others that might challenge him and then directed Paal to lead the group down into the grotto under Point Lookout and await his return. With any luck, the serenity of the cavern would isolate them from the virulent waves of energy affecting their minds while he dealt with whoever, or whatever, was sending them.

Once he was sure they had gone deep enough and were not coming back, he set off for the grove, hoping he wasn't already too late.

Nightblade pulsed vigorously in anticipation.

At long last his patience was being rewarded, and the aura of imminent victory was intoxicating.

In keeping the intrepid shell warrior occupied with the scaled folk, the Cree Lord was able to remain undetected, secretly assailing the unicorn with the honey collectors and eavesdropping on their activities. The latter had resulted in information that convinced him he must alter his timetable.

For days he remained hidden in the shadows, passively subverting the girl's reckless attempts at activating the gate, draining the portal's eldritch energy for himself as soon as she summoned it. A true aril would have realized right away they were being thwarted on purpose, but the untrained girl could only conclude that she was simply not skilled enough to activate the gate.

However, he could also see that his efforts to impede the witchling were having unintended consequences. Like offering two cubs one bone so they would tug at it and strengthen their jaws, his resistance provided the exact training ground the half breed needed to hone the mental acuity required for spell casting and, presumably, control over a gate.

Certainly he had hoped for more time to recharge his frein, but discovering that unicorns could not grow their precious horns in the human realm was a call to action—he had to feed on the young unicorn before the steed's magic faded or its flesh and blood would no longer help him regain the physical form he required to pass through the portal and get home.

Thus, when her sire and the unicorn foolishly believed her safe and left her in the grove alone, Nightblade knew it was time to strike; for though the endgame had been set in motion sooner than he anticipated, such were the Cree Chieftain's manipulations that it had come no faster than he was prepared for.

Lurking in the shadows of the grove wall, he waited as the witchling sat down to concentrate, then gently nudged her focus to where it needed to be, convincing the half breed that she had brought the portal to life all by herself.

Swaying in anticipation, he watched the eldritch charge flit from stone to stone. Thus far he had been taking small sips; now he would drink deep.

The rune energy required for teleportation was immense: if he could enter the gate as he had done to stop the unicorn from going home and stay there, he hoped to maximize his frein for the battles soon to be fought. It would be painful. Being caught in a gate had killed countless others and might even destroy him.

So be it. Nightblade was decided. One way or another, this must be the end of his exile on Earther.

To acquire as much energy as possible, he had to wait for the gate to reach prime aperture, which meant the portal would be open, and if it was open too long, a platoon of aril soldiers might come through and investigate. Therefore, his strike had to be precise.

Alas for the offspring, if there was one thing that defined Nightblade more than malice, it was precision.

Unaccustomed as she was to wielding her frein in any capacity beyond speaking with animals, the half breed fatigued easily after he revealed himself, and passed out.

Now, with the gate energy coursing through his insubstantial bones, he could manifest for more than enough time to surprise and slay the spikeless unicorn.

But first things first: the half breed was in danger, so no doubt all three of his enemies would soon be on their way. If they weren't already.

Fortunately, the shell warrior's lair under the ruined aril tower was closer to the gate than the witchling's dwelling, placing the pieces on the board in a perfect position for him to face and defeat his enemies one at a time. Just in case, the Cree Lord sent out some extra encouragement, a summoning call to the scale folk, urging them to join him in the grove.

As expected, and according to plan, Nightblade did not have long to wait before his thoughts were drawn away from the pleasure of scheming by a heavy thump, marking the arrival of his jevaled foe.

"Perfect," Nightblade murmured, tightening into a boulder-sized cloud of eyes and teeth. "Though the variables be upended, the outcome once again propels me closer to my goals."

A flash of whistling silver was his only reply.

The Cree Lord filled with mirth, prepared to scoff at the foolish assault. But instead of passing through him, the staff struck him a searing jolt that sent him sizzling across the clearing like a batted acorn. Nightblade sped through the air in shock until he was halted by the unyielding weave of the grove wall and burst into a shower of sparks. Shapeshifting amid the embers, Nightblade coalesced into a distorted quadruped. "You strike me in my incorporeal form?" he growled. "Impossible!"

The menacing shell warrior tilted his head. "Not for such as I. Who are you? And to what foul purpose are you set upon?"

"Who am I?" Nightblade's guttural whisper was laced with malice. "One who shall soon take his vengeance upon you and your Maker's witchling."

"So it's true." Taliko shook his head in disbelief. "After all this time, the Maker's enemies renew their feud."

The shadow form let slip a sinister, knowing laugh and began to change.

Taliko's eyes narrowed, watching closely for an attack as the shifting mass refined its aspect from paw to maw. When the visage of his old foe was finally revealed, Taliko sucked in a startled breath and rocked back on his heels. "What deviltry is this?" the shell warrior cried. "Saber fangs I see, teeth like I have not seen since the Cree Chieftain strode the mountain. Yet he I saw destroyed, and generations to come and go before another should rise to take his place. So the Maker told me."

"So the Maker told you?" Nightblade laughed. "Your witch-maker lied. Indeed, I am he you waged war on once before, for the Cree Chieftain cannot be destroyed in this magic dead realm. Even now, thanks to the witchling's untrained attempts to open the portal, my spectral paws grow closer to treading the ground once more, and quite soon my bloodthirsty howl will teach these humans the true meaning of terror."

"Reborn?" Taliko's nostrils flared. "How?"

Nightblade laughed off the question with a dark growl. "Be assured, without your Maker's help, I shall carve that shell from your back until the magic that molds you bursts. When your friends arrive, there will be nothing left of your existence but my paw print in your dust coil."

The enemies locked eyes, the tension-primed silence between them thick with the unbridled menace of their saber teeth, the black fangs of the Cree Chieftain slicing down to the ground, and the ivory incisors of the shell warrior curving up toward the sun above.

The confident Cree Lord moved first, shattering the standoff without warning, his breathtaking speed made all the more frightening by the utter silence of his assault.

Taliko somersaulted up and over the sudden attack with panther-like reflexes.

Against anyone else those combat instincts would have vaulted him to safety, but not against the Nightblade.

Rearing up on his hind legs the Cree Lord ripped into Taliko's tail with his fearsome teeth, filling the appendage with icy venom before it could streak away overhead.

Agility compromised by the sudden numbness in his tail, the reptilian landed with a crash and tumbled over several times.

Nightblade never stopped moving. Like a wave hitting a wall, he was already surging back in the opposite direction before Taliko found his feet. Seeing the reptile facing away from him, Nightblade readied to clamp his deadly fangs on the wounded tail and flip the turtle on his back.

Yet just as his teeth arrived, the shell warrior side-rolled and brought the silver tip of his bo-staff to bear, impaling Nightblade between the jaws.

Reacting instantly to Nightblade's shadow essence, the blessed silver plunged down the chieftain's throat like a flaming fist.

Though empowered as he was by the rune energy of the gate, the shocking, unexpected charge of the magic staff was still too strong for Nightblade, and he exploded like a firework.

The sparking vapors of Nightblade's tattered wolfen aspect fell back to Earth slowly, and both combatants used the respite to gather themselves: Taliko to thump life back into his lower extremities and Nightblade to pool his energy and thoughts.

The blond witch must have suspected I cannot be slain here, the Cree Lord seethed to himself. *Why else would she have given this vile jevaling a weapon that can strike my shadow form and drain the frein from my physical form?* Nightblade glared at the ivory staff in Taliko's claws. *This thing is a champion's weapon. A king's weapon. How had a mere Sentinel even come in possession of such an artifact?*

Variables for another time.

He had thought the possibility of a draining prolonged conflict with the shell warrior unlikely. Still, it had been prepared for.

Time then to employ the tactics of the hypocritical aril, who so despise killing but think nothing of engaging others to do the job for them, just as they did in sending me through the gate on that moonless night so many years ago.

The pair circled each other.

Painfully aware of the Cree Chieftain's great speed, Taliko kept his knees bent, ready to spring and meet him midleap, where he could once again use his staff like a lance. Watching carefully, he waited for the wolf lord's rippling muscles to tense.

Charging, however, was not Nightblade's intention, not while he was maneuvering his enemy into position.

The moment the shell warrior stood where he wanted him, the Cree Chieftain snarled, "Attack!" and the great reptile found himself swarmed over from behind by a quintet of lizardlings hiding in the grove wall.

Taliko rolled with the assault, casting his assailants away easily.

"Zil!" the shell warrior spat before he had even turned to look. "I afforded you safety. In choosing to rejoin your diabolical Maker, you and your companions force my hand."

"Force your hand?" Nightblade howled with amusement. "They never had a choice. This was my plan all along. To keep you occupied and away from your duty while I fed off rune energy and my bloodthirsty honey collectors."

"Growing stronger and stronger in the process," Taliko surmised. "Your cunning knows no bounds, Cree Chieftain."

"Indeed," Nightblade agreed. "I confess to being surprised that you have somehow hidden away most of my jevaled minions, but no matter. Enough have come, and they shall lead me to the others.

"Step forth, my little ones, and let's show this construct what our manipulations have wrought."

Transfixed by the jevaling magic on display before him, Taliko couldn't help but watch as the Cree Lord pulsed dark, noxious fumes into the lizardlings.

Doubling their mass, evolving them well beyond their wiry three-foot frames into five feet of formidable muscle.

"Now," Nightblade hissed when the making was complete, "destroy him."

The quintet broke apart, seeking to surround Taliko. Seeing this caused him no great alarm, however. Instead, it was the sight of Paal, limping through the grove wall and over to the Cree as well.

"No Paal!" Taliko cried, fending off an onslaught of blows from every angle. "Not you!"

Paal glanced back at him once, then stepped into Nightblade's embrace to be doused in ebony eldritch mist. When the vapors dissipated, Paal too was bigger, thicker, and more muscular than before, but unlike the others he had also fallen to his knees, eyes shut tight.

"Rise," the Cree Chieftain whispered. "I have made you strong. Join your brothers. Slay the shell warrior and feast on his gravelly flesh."

Paal opened his eyes, and with the help of a spear that was now too small for him, rose unsteadily to his clawed feet.

"Fight it Paal!" Taliko shouted. "Your mind is stronger now too! Strong enough to resist!"

Paal's glassy gaze settled on the battle, and he took a swaying step forward, breaking Taliko's heart.

Though he felt both affection and friendship for the humans, they were warm-blooded. Milk-bred. He was egg-born. Reptilian. And had worked hard with the lizardlings, hoping for some truer kinship.

Taliko knew that even if he survived this confrontation, losing Paal meant he would soon lose the others as well. In trying to save the lizardlings, he had also been tricked into neglecting his duty to watch over Casey at all times, and now it had been for nothing. Wrapped together, his failures struck him a blow deep in the soul like no physical strike could have.

Sensing his faltering spirit, the enhanced lizardlings rushed forward, and it was all the shell warrior could do to keep them at bay.

For the first time in his life, Taliko wanted to flee. If only he could pick up Casey and race through the wall out of the grove. StarFall could do it, but the steed was a true being of light and nature, while Taliko was merely a jevaled soldier.

After several leaden steps, Paal stopped at the edge of the battlefront, his head drooping.

"Destroy him!" Nightblade commanded, and Paal's head snapped up.

Despite being under siege from multiple opponents, Taliko heard Nightblade's order and risked a glance toward Paal. It was only a moment, but long enough to make eye contact and see the lizardling's evergreen orbs were still glazed with indecision.

"Fight it Paal!" Taliko cried again.

Paal blinked, and Taliko saw his eyes change, filling not with madness—but furious resolve!

"Yes Paal!" Taliko whispered as the lizardling leaped upon Zil's back and tackled him to the ground.

"What is this?" the Cree Chieftain hissed. "A traitor to your own kind!"

Nightblade tensed, ready to pounce and tear the defiant minion limb from limb.

Then he calmed himself.

Lowering his gaze, Nightblade railed quietly, cursing the unpredictable nature of jevaling magic. As much as he wanted to vent his frustration by snapping the wayward pawn out of existence with quick snap of his jaws, that was not the plan. He had to let the scale folk do their task and save his remaining frein to confront the juvenile and the human with his physical form.

Seeking to rend him with their teeth and claws, the lizardlings surrounding Taliko stormed forward in unison.

Taliko leaped into the charge behind his bo-staff, striking his closest assailant in the chest and then using his momentum to vault beyond the coordinated attack.

Twisting in midair, he landed behind them and swiftly stormed into the still-standing trio. "For the Maker!" he growled with renewed verve, striking his enemy on the left in the jaw with his staff and then turning to batter the next with the back of his shell. Coming full circle, he prepared to unleash a rib-crunching blow to the midsection of the third.

But the last surprised him with his readiness. Launching itself from one of the tree stump chairs, the lizard delivered a smashing headbutt to Taliko's chest just as he completed his turn.

The ferocious blow drove the wind from Taliko's lungs and sent his weapon twirling away.

"For the Maker," the lizardling hissed in his ear. Then the pair tumbled off in a biting, slashing tangle of tooth and claw.

Across the clearing Zil reached back, dug his claws into Paal's shoulder scales, and tossed him over his head with one hand. The lizardling crashed into the unforgiving marble of the nearest gate pillar with a heavy thud that nearly broke his back.

Expecting a follow-up attack, Paal rolled over, shook his head, and rose unsteadily to his feet to meet it.

The attack did not come.

Thankful for the respite but wondering what Zil might be up to, he glanced warily at his opponent.

When their eyes met, Zil shocked him with the ability to speak. "I am the obvious master here. You are cunning; join me, and I will make you my second as we serve the Maker."

Paal took a deep breath that helped him gather his thoughts. A moment later he was amazed to find words of his own hissing over his tongue: "The Maker is powerful, but he opposes the natural balance. I am thankful for his gifts, but he is not worthy of our servitude."

Having been born far and away the tallest and thickest of limb in the clan, Zil growled and drew himself up to his full six-foot height. Towering now over Paal by nearly a foot, his intimidating might set the smaller lizardling's heart panic-racing. "And so," Zil hissed, "you will spite the Maker by serving his shell-bound foe?"

Paal shook his head from left to right, sidestepping slowly off the dais, away from Casey and toward the thick green of the grove wall. "I will serve no one," he replied. "Instead, I shall seek to live and work in harmony with those around me, as we did before the Maker."

Zil laughed. "You fool! Can you not see? We have risen! Risen above the wings and paws that preyed upon us! With the touch of the Maker, we no longer need to serve the environment. The environment can serve us! We must seize that opportunity! We were weak. Nearly mindless. Now we are strong. Where once we ate the cricket, now we shall feast on any flesh we desire. That is the natural order of things."

At that Zil looked over toward Casey.

"No," Paal said evenly. In search of a weapon, he reached back slowly toward the wall, and his heart skipped a beat when a branch slipped into his hand as readily as if the Gategrove itself had given it to him. "I will not allow it."

"You will not allow it?"

Zil tossed his head back and laughed heartily, then abruptly surged forward in an effort to catch Paal by surprise.

Paal brought the club around to smash Zil in the jaw, but the bigger lizardling blocked it away easily with one hand and seized him by the throat with the other.

"We are too few," Zil hissed, digging his claws into Paal's neck, "and so I had hoped you would join us. We lizardlings shall prosper under the Maker and rewrite the natural order of this entire mountain. Since you have seen fit to reject that destiny, I give you the honor of being the first victim of my new age."

Not far away Taliko and his assailant rolled to a halt. Flipping up to his feet with an elegant whirl, Taliko rotated his hips into a tail whip. The added torque put so much power into the attack that it smashed into the lizardling's jaw and broke it.

However, using his injured appendage to deliver such a devastating blow was not without cost, and Taliko wobbled, blinded by a fierce flash of agony. When his eyes cleared, the shell warrior saw his foe standing in shock opposite him, mouth flapping uselessly, and felt a momentary pang of sadness at what he had been forced to do.

The moment passed, and straightening the razor-sharp claws of his left hand into a lethal wedge, Taliko finished the miserable creature off with a swift slash across the throat.

Just then he heard Zil telling Paal how he would rewrite the natural order of the mountain and make him the first victim of his new age.

The threat brought to mind his discussion with Jonas about harmony and peace, and he realized that if Nightblade and Zil won this battle, all the work he and Jonas had done to conquer the Cave of Bones would be for naught.

Movement drew his focus back to the present.

His remaining opponents had recovered, and using his distraction had begun creeping up on him from opposite angles.

In their enhanced state, they were proving to be much craftier and deadlier than before, and Taliko knew he was now as vulnerable to their claws as they were to his. Without his bo-staff, he wasn't sure if he could fend off all three of them at the same time.

But he was about to find out.

Zil brought his other hand to Paal's throat, but before he could bite him, Paal wedged his cudgel into the back of the jawline, where his assailant didn't have any teeth.

Zil hissed in frustration. He could not bite and would have to take his hands from Paal's throat to remove the obstacle, freeing his enemy. But thinking he still had the advantage, Zil squeezed his claws tighter. If he couldn't bite Paal, he would choke the life from him and tear him to pieces afterward for the sheer pleasure of it.

Paal panic-twisted, then, still learning how to use his new body, realized suddenly that his foe had miscalculated and brought up his eviscerating toe claws to rake Zil's chest.

Zil roared in fury but did not let go. Instead, he used both hands to raise Paal as high as he could and body slammed him to the ground. The move momentarily dislodged the branch from his mouth, but just as Zil's jaws were about to tear into his throat, Paal brought the club around a second time and just managed to keep the snapping teeth at bay.

Growling in triumph because the wedge was no longer in the fleshy part of his jawline, Zil clamped his teeth up and down on the branch until it splintered down the middle.

Once more the deadly teeth came for his throat, and once more Paal let his instincts tell him what to do: in a flash he slammed the ends of the broken club against either side of Zil's skull as hard as he could, stunning him.

Seizing the moment, Paal slithered out of Zil's clutches with serpentine speed and got behind him, then used the larger half of the broken cudgel to engage a choke hold on the bigger reptile's muscled neck.

Coming to his senses, Zil began to thrash and roll, trying to dislodge Paal, but he was still reeling from the effects of the concussive head blow and his strength quickly faded. Even so, Paal feared that he lacked the brute power to finish the job until finally, Zil collapsed.

With a great sigh, Paal clambered up to his feet and caught his breath. Once his eyes cleared of blood lust, he saw Taliko fighting against his brethren.

Feeling an urge to assist him, Paal willed his feet forward, but the very first step sent him swaying recklessly into one of the wooden benches facing the swan sculpture and, ultimately, headfirst into the pond.

Meanwhile, the shell warrior could do little more than remain on the defensive, keeping the lizardlings at bay with well-timed lunges and vicious tail swipes and slowly working his way back to his bo-staff. To his dismay, however, the lizardlings soon realized his plan and fell back, covering each other until they could toss the hateful staff farther away.

Watching his weapon land in the pond and sink out of sight, Taliko sighed. "I suppose we'll have to do this the hard way."

Too late perhaps, Taliko understood how much he had come to rely on his weapon more than was wise. He was still stronger, but the enhanced lizardlings were much quicker than he. They also learned swiftly from their mistakes, creating a true struggle to devise a tactic to defeat an enemy that knew well enough to strike quickly and dart back beyond his reach. They were wearing him down, and they all knew it.

Then Taliko heard a soulful keen that sped his heart.

After falling into the pond and lying in it for a long minute, Paal was revived by the tingling sensation of the cool, refreshing water washing over his scales. Then a splash disturbed the underwater quiet surrounding him, and he turned to see the shell warrior's bo-staff sinking beside him.

Paal blinked in surprise, then quickly stood and began to twirl it like he had seen Taliko do, making the weapon sing its war cry. Having thus caught the turtle's attention, he hurled it in his direction.

Taliko didn't know if it was his work with the lizardlings or Paal's utter hatred for Zil that had allowed him to break free of the Cree Chieftain's hold, but he was happy for the outcome and seized the staff in midair with one hand when it reached him.

Taliko leveled his gaze.

"Now we shall see," he said, and no sooner had the words scraped out of his mouth than he spun into an attack, bringing the heavy silver crown of his staff down with a bone-splitting crunch on a lizardling kneecap, sending the reptile writhing to the ground.

Hoping to tip the great turtle on his back, one of his lithe opponents immediately seized the opportunity to scramble up on his shell. The lizardling miscalculated the great power of Taliko's limbs, however, and the shell warrior didn't falter a bit with the extra weight.

Undeterred, the creature dug his rear claws into the thick shell for balance and slashed and dug at the back of Taliko's neck, trying to decapitate him.

Taliko needed just a moment to pry the creature off his back, but the remaining lizardling kept feinting frontal assaults to give his companion the chance he needed to deliver a mortal blow.

Breathing heavily, feeling the claws at his throat beginning to pierce his armored skin, Taliko whirled his tail around in an effort to swat the third into unconsciousness, or at least far enough away that he could get the creature off his back before his companion recovered. But this time his strike was anticipated, and moving like a cobra, the lizardling sank his jagged teeth into the limb and held on.

Taliko snarled happily; he would gladly suffer more pain in his tail to remove the strangling lizard on his back and quickly wedged his bo-staff over his shoulder to dislodge him.

Sensing what Taliko was about to do, the lizardling raked at his face with its free hand. Fighting off the attack with his left hand, Taliko worked the staff like a lever with his right to flip the creature away.

Only then did he realize he'd been tricked.

The claws in his face had been a distraction to get him to use only one hand while the clever lizardling used his remaining three limbs to get a firm grasp on the staff. When Taliko flicked the lizard away, he failed to compensate for the overweighted end—and the weapon yanked from his grip and flew away with his foe.

Momentarily stunned at having lost his weapon yet again, and just as he felt the tide was turning in his favor, Taliko looked dazedly at his empty hands.

Sensing the shell warrior's despondence, the crafty lizardling clinging to his tail seized the opportunity to scamper up his back and resume the attack on his throat.

Vision clouding with primitive rage, Taliko clenched his fists. There was nothing to do now but hope for the best with what he was about to do next.

Turning his back away from Casey, he dug in with his rear claws and concentrated on the eldritch energy housed in his chest, harnessing and channeling it into his shell cavity.

The building energy filled his eyes with a topaz glow and set the bottom of his shell alight with spectral yellow-gold radiance. Taliko grunted, resetting his feet as the ethereal light swirled up and around his shell until it was completely lit, indicating the charge was primed for release.

Bathed suddenly in eldritch light, the lizardling on his back stopped attacking and stared at the golden glow in confused fascination.

The shell blinked twice, then pulsed, unleashing a soul-sheering wave of sound and fury that hurled the lizardling into the air before it could even scream.

The careening reptile smashed into the upper edge of the looming tree line, moving with such speed that the tightly woven branches acted like a solid wall that shattered his spine even as it impaled him.

Though he'd braced himself with his sturdy legs, unleashing his shock wave required the anchoring of all five of his appendages; thus Taliko went skidding across the glade in the opposite direction to crash into the far wall himself, albeit with much less devastating impact.

The unprepared were far less fortunate.

The lizardling that had stolen his staff and his ally with the shattered knee were blown across the grove, the former to crack his skull against one of the sturdy tree stump seats around the pond, the latter to disappear under the collapsing shelter Jonas had built.

Paal dug into the edge of the pond with what strength he had left, but soon found himself sliding across the grass and then airborne until he was miraculously caught in a bed of soft pine needles hidden in the grove wall. There he remained, pinned some six feet off the ground until the wave subsided and he fell in a heap.

Though shielded somewhat by a gate pillar and Taliko's attempt to aim his shell blast in the opposite direction, Casey was still swept from the dais with cruel indifference.

Scooping her up where she lay, the merciless sonic wave bounced her roughly down the stairs and sent her tumbling over the ground like a broken doll until she became wedged against the base of the grove wall.

What happened to Nightblade could never have been anticipated by anyone in the Gategrove that day…

Hoping tightly woven winds would deflect the sonic surge around him, the wolf lord tried to defend himself by coalescing into a seven-foot-tall tornado. Instead, the sonic wave merged with the cold shadow spiral he had become and set fire to him on a molecular level.

In that instant every filament of the Cree Chieftain blazed with excruciating pain—like his very soul was on fire. His ethereal scream was so great that every living creature within a hundred miles felt a psychic twinge knife into their temple for several seconds.

Bristling with unharnessed magical fury, the turbulent vortex that was

Nightblade swiftly began to grow, its cyclonic rage buffeting everything in the Gategrove with hurricane-force winds.

Taliko looked on it in awe as it swelled over to over twenty feet high, then exploded in a shower of indigo and green sparks.

Still racing with cyclonic energy, the swirling magical embers bounced off the grove's tree line in countless directions, razing Taliko's leathery skin like white-hot flaming darts until he was forced to find solitude within his shell.

Gradually the glistening needles slowed, drawn as if by a great magnet to come together in a flaming constellation of muscle, bone, and sinew that resembled the Cree Chieftain's wolfen aspect. When the constellation was complete, it flared brightly with eldritch light, green at the edges, purple at its heart.

Golden embers appeared in its body, and the flaming wolf howled, its terrible cry lingering on and on as the flares blazed through its figure as if on fuses, carving the Cree Chieftain from eldritch flame into flesh and blood.

"You…" Nightblade panted at last, sparks still rippling through its rich ebony fur like tiny shards of lightning. "What have you done?" A wave of stunned hate poured from his green eyes. "My frein…is overflowing, but it burns, down to my soul."

Never have I seen or heard song of such a thing, Nightblade thought in a rage, *that a jevaled warrior should be so infused with innate power that it could restore the frein of a Maker! And so, at long last, I understand how the witch tricked and defeated me when I thought her finished.*

Though beset himself by painful injuries and battle fatigue, Taliko rose to his feet, and with a wary eye cast at the saber-toothed wolf, limped toward his staff.

"You are truly an abomination," continued Nightblade, eyes bright with jade flames. "If the aril lords discover what your Maker has done by creating you, they will give her the Nectar of the Nora'ah.

Trying not to look as tired as he felt, Taliko picked up his weapon. He did not know what the Nectar of Nora'ah was, but it sounded like a poison of some kind.

Deciding not to address it, Taliko returned, "And you should be dead."

Nightblade shook his head. *You do not even know your own power*, the Cree Lord considered silently. *How can this be?* Aloud he said, "I cannot be destroyed here; this I told you already."

"Why are you here at all!" Taliko cried. "The Maker suggested you made a bargain of some sort, but what grievance can be worth this?"

Nightblade laughed. "You know so little of home that at last I understand. I thought all this time she brought you with her, but that is untrue. You are a denizen of this realm, making your creation all the more treasonous under the Aril Law. Oh how I hope she lives yet, so I can see her suffer."

Taliko stood straighter. "You have used jevaling magic in this realm as well. How is that any different?"

The great wolf stared at him, green fire flaring in his eye sockets. "I submit to no law but those of my own instincts. Such is my right as Cree Chieftain."

Sensing he was about to sway, Taliko drove his staff to the ground as if to emphasize his point. "Indeed, and so I ask you again. Cree Chieftain. Lord of your own people. Of what concern is this child to you? Why embark at all on this mission of murder? Let alone return from the edge of death to take it up again so many years later?"

Green eyes flickering, a menacing growl in his throat, Nightblade peered at the shell warrior for a long moment, saying nothing.

"You assume the bargain that sent you here still binds you in some way." Taliko nodded in understanding. "I know what foul outcome the aril seek. The mystery, is what is so valuable to the mighty Cree Chieftain that he committed to such an ill-fated pact for himself instead of sending a trusted member of his pack."

"I do not assume," Nightblade snorted, raising his nose to catch a distant scent.

The human is on his way, but…he comes alone! Thrice curse that cowardly unicorn for daring not to face me! Nightblade choked down an angry growl so as not to alert the shell warrior to his thoughts.

"After all this time?" Taliko asked mildly. "And no way of knowing if the terms of your agreement survive? Certainly you must."

In that instant Nightblade felt an alien sensation fill his heart.

Fear.

Could this cursed jevaling be right? The aril are long-lived; no doubt his ally was still in position, perhaps even risen to a more powerful place of prominence. But the passage of time did create uncertainty. The girl's death may have become meaningless.

No, not meaningless. In time, even if by accident, she will be able to open the gate herself, and the aril are too possessive and self-serving to allow that. Still, his ally may seize the time variable as an opportunity to renegotiate the agreed upon terms…

"Have my thoughts been useful to the Cree Chieftain?" Taliko asked.

Useful… Nightblade mused silently, his thoughts racing through new calculations of leverage and deceit. The hunt had changed direction, but such was his predatory edge that already the Cree Lord was compensating for it.

"Yes," Nightblade replied, snarling each syllable with distinction. "Yes, they have proved useful,"

They have convinced me you are more useful to me alive. If his ally foolishly sought to use the time variable to change the terms of their agreement, he needed leverage, and as an instrument of banned magic, the jevaling provided that. Taliko's creation alone was punishable by death. Knowing the aril, that meant they would try to hide it from the rest of Leutia—presenting him another chip to bargain with.

If he killed Taliko now, he would disappear into the ether, robbing him of the proof of his existence.

There was no way around it. Both the girl and Taliko must live. For now, at least until he could reaffirm the terms. The question was how to manipulate the delay into an advantage…

"The years have indeed been many," Nightblade mused aloud. "Perhaps you are right."

The Cree Chieftain fixed his eyes on Taliko. "My frein is filled to bursting with a power beyond even my ken. So as now an immutable fate-victorious aligns with me, and this thanks to you, I shall offer you a mercy, and a vow, in compensation for your usefulness.

"The blood of the unicorn will be mine. However, should the witchling agree to open the gate so I can go home, we shall part for now in peace. Shall she refuse, then I destroy the witchling, her sire, and you, and begin a reign of terror from this mountain the likes of which Earther has never seen."

Nightblade vanished.

Taliko blinked in surprise, then crouched into attack position when the Cree reappeared hovering over Casey's prone form. Despite his menacing aspect, however, Taliko's heart raced with fear. There was simply no way he could get to the enemy before he struck a lethal blow on the unconscious girl.

"Urge the humans to choose wisely…Taliko." Nightblade looked down at Casey and placed a heavy paw on her chest. "My fangs have returned to the shadows, and continued conflict with me will surely lead to your destruction.

"But," the Cree Chieftain's tone softened, and his eyes rose to meet Taliko's, "this ending need not be sung. You live well here. Don't waste what remains of it. Convince the humans to sacrifice the unicorn and send me home. Do as I ask, and I shall leave to you the fate of the lizardlings. Egg-born like you, they are the closest thing to a pack you shall ever have. Much closer than the humans could ever be. Do as I ask, and all of you finish your lives as fate decrees. Do it not"—the growl seeped back into Nightblade's throat—"further my exile in this forsaken realm, and the numbering of every Earther's days is left to me."

Nightblade's eyes flared a moment, then he disappeared.

Taliko sucked a startled breath through his teeth and leaned into a ready stance. When the wolf lord did not return, he exhaled sadly and scampered over to Casey as fast as his weary limbs would carry him.

A quick check revealed that though the girl had been battered, bruised, and burned during the clash of sabers unfolding around her, she was still breathing normally. Taliko surmised that being unconscious and limp may have actually helped her ride out the sonic wave without serious injury, and being blown to the clearing's edge had miraculous taken her out of the path of the flaming embers racing around the Gategrove.

The shell warrior shook his head and sat. When he and the Maker had laid their trap for Nightblade, his sonic wave had powered her frein so she could remain hidden long enough to perform a complex spell that normally took many casters to weave. Taliko had asked then if it would also not energize Nightblade, and she assured him it would not. That it could not, because his powers came from the shadow frein while hers came from the golden frein. The two could not mix. And yet, somehow, today, Taliko had aided Nightblade. Something that should be impossible.

A noise from the ruined shelter drew his attention. Recalling that one of Nightblade's minions had been hurled into it by his shell blast, Taliko vaulted over to it in several long strides. A moment later the lizardling with the broken kneecap limped forward and fell to the ground before him.

"Master," the lizardling began, but suddenly Paal was beside him and said, "His name is not master; his name is Lord Taliko."

Taliko looked at Paal for a moment, absorbing the honorific he had just been given. With it Paal was making a clear distinction between "leader" and "master," the former implying choice and the latter servitude. It made sense, and perhaps he should reflect on it himself as it regarded his own Maker. Time for that later. The rebellious lizardling had to be dealt with now.

"Lord Taliko," the lizardling began again. "I ask for mercy."

"Why did you abandon your brothers and join Zil?" Taliko asked.

After staring at the ground a moment, the creature raised its aqua-colored head and regarded him sadly. "This I did not want to do, but Zil forced his companions to take me."

Taliko glanced at Paal skeptically and then back at the lizardling before him. "And why should he choose you? Or force you at all? Unlike Paal, you seemed to me a very willing combatant during the conflict."

"He said he would destroy me if I did not come. Zil chose me because I am one of only three who could help him start a new clan."

"A new clan?"

"Lord Taliko, this is Liss," Paal offered. "Back in the cave, Zil and I argued. Then it was that his followers struck me from behind. Believing I was unconscious, they dragged me into a corner. I was but dazed, yet lied still to recover my strength and decide when best to strike. While I did so, what she says I saw with my own eyes before trailing them here to the Gategrove. True it is as well that she is one of but three females in our clan."

Taliko's eyes widened. He had been totally oblivious. "I see," he said simply. After a moment he added, "Zil was certainly craftier than I gave him credit for. Brave of you to set out after him. Without your help this battle may have gone very differently. You have my thanks. What do you say, Paal, as regards the fate of Liss?"

Paal stared hard at Liss for several long moments. Then redirected his serpentine gaze toward Zil lying sprawled on the ground, and finally back to Taliko. "I think there has been enough killing today, Lord Taliko."

Taliko nodded and stepped forward, helping Liss to her feet. "Well said Paal." Taliko agreed. Then he placed Liss's hand in Paal's. "I place her in your charge Paal. If you deem she becomes unworthy of the clan, it will be up to you and the others to decide her fate, be it death or to climb the mountain and live out her days in solitude. Do you accept the charge I give you?"

"I do Lord Taliko."

"Very well. Go now and return to the cave. Be sure the others are safe and well. I shall join you when I can, after I have seen to matters here."

Paal and Liss nodded and left the grove.

Taliko glanced at Casey. Best not to disturb her before she awoke and could tell him if she was in pain. Instead, he retrieved the bedroll from the smashed shelter and made her as comfortable as he could.

Taliko took a deep breath and let it out in a rush.

Jonas and StarFall would be here soon. Then he would have to tell his story. How ironic, he thought, that just a week after Jonas had to confess, it would be his turn.

Taliko could see no other way. Not after this. He would have to break his promise to the Maker and tell Jonas the truth.

About how he'd truly come to be here.

About Nightblade.

And how he'd just put them all in graver danger than ever.

10
UNEXPECTED GUESTS

Jonas had just finished rubbing down Rebel and getting him into his stall when he heard the distinctive sonic thunderclap that he knew could only be Taliko.

The rancher took three steps toward the barn door, then stumbled when a surge of pain struck him behind the eyes. Shaking his head to clear it, he looked in the direction of the Gategrove and a strong sense that something was wrong settled over him. But what? Casey in the Gategrove? Taliko battling the lizardlings? Or had Thunder Peak just thrust some new danger upon them?

StarFall came up from behind and steered him out the door. One glance at the steed and he could see the panic in his eyes. He could also see the wound in his forehead, oozing and bubbling now as if it were under a low campfire boil.

"Whoa, whoa!" Jonas said urgently but without raising his voice. "Hold on." he raised his hands in a stopping gesture. "StarFall, wait."

The fledgling unicorn rose to his hind legs in irritation, knocking Jonas to the ground. Bending low, the animal nudged him several times with his forehead, snorting and whinnying, not letting him stand and conveying his anger.

When StarFall finally retreated, Jonas was furious. "Are you done?" he yelled, getting his feet under him. "That's my little girl out there, and you are wasting my time!"

Jonas strode up to StarFall, and when the horse did not back up, their faces bumped.

Jonas drew a hand across his forehead, smearing it with StarFall's blood, and held it up to the steed's silver eye. "You see this? This is you! Bleeding! Look at this!" Jonas held out his shirt, red with the unicorn's blood from the head butt StarFall used to knock him to the ground. "StarFall wait! Jonas go!"

The filly he had brought back with him from Widow Dorn's barn wandered out behind them, and Jonas pointed at her. "StarFall. Heal!"

StarFall looked at the other horse, then back to Jonas, and lowered his head softly on Jonas's shoulder.

"I know," Jonas said, patting his neck. "You're worried about Casey. So am I. But you can't help her, or us, if you don't take care of yourself first."

Jonas stepped away.

In the next instant, he pulled his pistol, sighted a tree some twenty yards away and fired upon it, striking the bark nearly center twice in a row.

StarFall snorted in surprise and cantered back.

Jonas drew a deep breath. Then, holding the smoking gun in the air for him to see clearly, he turned around to face StarFall. "Jonas. Ready," he said firmly.

StarFall looked back at him with a mixed gaze of fear and confidence.

"Don't worry." Jonas twirled and then holstered his gun. "Jonas ready."

"Now," he continued softly. "Jonas go. StarFall heal and get better." He pointed back and forth between StarFall and Bonnie several times.

With a resigned snort and a shake of his head, StarFall turned and whinnied softly to Bonnie, who followed him back into the barn.

"Right then," Jonas said, scampering into the woods at a quick trot. "Good luck to both of us."

Since arriving in Storm Town, Jonas rarely wore boots. To him they seemed cumbersome and uncomfortable. When Sheriff Tanner deputized him, he put on boots and spurs because they just seemed expected, but most all other times he wore the moccasins Mae had given him.

They were comfortable and magical, just like Casey's.

Of course, Mae had never actually told him them they were magical (or blessed, as she sometimes referred to the pearlwood and the apple trees of the Tamm Orchard). He always meant to ask her, but…but he knew they were just the same. While wearing them he felt lighter and faster. Much faster. In his moccasins he could get to the Gategrove in almost half the time. The spring in his step was already strong, but while wearing the brown leather foot-cuffs he could also jump noticeably higher over roots, rocks, shrubs, and other obstacles.

So he had always guessed, but once Casey showed up wearing them, he knew for sure. Jonas didn't know how, but they never ripped, never tore or wore out. And each day when he saw her tug them on by the door, it seemed certain that their just-big-enough perfect fit would be outgrown the very next morning. But over the course of fourteen years, it never happened, and Jonas only knew one word to describe it: magic.

Jonas wondered briefly if he could catch Casey without her moccasins on. He couldn't catch Mae, that he knew for sure, so he doubted it. Breathing deeply and sweating under the August sunshine, Jonas crouched down in sight of Point Lookout and remembered frolicking in these very same woods and streams with Mae. How she could so easily disappear among the trees, and the delightful laugh behind him when she was ready to be found. They were some of the best memories he had.

Having caught his breath, and sighting no battle and no movement, he dashed from stone to stone across the sparkling stream diving under Point Lookout and sprinted toward the grove.

A steady burst of shift-scampering followed, and then Jonas was threading his way through the Gategrove wall and into the clearing they protected, some forty minutes after he had left StarFall.

He entered the clearing, gun drawn, to find Taliko sitting quietly, warding over Casey, who lay on the ground with her eyes closed.

"What happened?" Jonas rushed over. "Is she all right?"

Taliko nodded from the edge of the dais, scratching at the dirt with his bo-staff. "Casey is well. The bruises you see are mostly my fault. She was unconscious when I arrived. The foe and his allies were waiting for me. The tide of battle turned against me, and I was forced to use my shell blast to win the day. She awoke briefly, and I gave her some tingle tea. Now she rests."

Jonas had been bending down, checking over Casey's injuries for himself. Satisfied, he stood and looked at Taliko, barely containing his pent-up fury over Taliko's weeklong absence. "Fighting off what enemies? Something came through the gate? Please don't tell me it was those lizardlings again."

The pair stared at each other quietly for a long moment until Jonas drew his hand over his face in exasperation. "Taliko…"

"Nightblade," Taliko answered.

"What's a Nightblade?" Jonas snapped.

"Just as the unicorns are to horses, the Cree are to wolves. Nightblade is their chieftain. Cunning. Powerful. And shortly after Casey was delivered to you, he came through the gate on a mission to slay her. The Maker and I thought we had destroyed the beast, but it appears we were mistaken."

"The Maker?" Jonas's eyes widened. "Mae? You and Mae fought this creature? And where was I during all this? Why didn't you come for me? Why didn't she come for me?"

Taliko took a deep breath. "It is the true story of my coming, not the lie you have believed since our meeting."

"Lie?" Jonas echoed. "You mean the story about Mae sneaking you through the gate to bring me our baby?"

Taliko nodded.

Jonas looked about the grove for a moment, taking in the smashed shelter and upturned earth that hinted at a frenzied battle with many combatants. His eyes lingered on the oversized lizardling impaled at the top of the grove wall.

Then he looked at Casey, resting comfortably near Taliko, who was not without injuries—some of them serious, by the look of his damaged tail.

Feeling much of the anger drain from him, he took a seat on the dais near his daughter's head. With Taliko stationed at her feet, the duo formed a pair of wistful bookend guardians. "I can't be too surprised, I suppose," he grumbled, "Not after lying to Casey myself all these years."

Jonas paused to glance down at his daughter with a warm smile. "Reckon I do understand the need for secrets sometimes, and the power they can have over you."

Taliko nodded quietly in agreement.

"Right then." Jonas folded his arms and looked sideways at his reptilian friend. "Whereabouts you've been fussing? And what happened here? Let's have it."

Casey moaned softly and pushed herself up to her elbows. "Have what?" she mumbled.

Jonas and Taliko jumped to their feet in surprise.

"Casey!" Jonas knelt beside her. "Are you okay? What happened? Taliko said you were unconscious when he got here."

"The gate!" Casey tried to scurry to her feet but needed Jonas to steady her. "The gate…" Her eyes took in the scarred earth and ruined shelter. "What in seven bells happened to that?"

"If you are able, perhaps we should talk as we go?" Taliko suggested. "It will be getting dark soon."

"Good idea." Jonas agreed.

After navigating the grove wall, they began the trek toward home. Along the way Casey detailed the opening of the gate, the mysterious cloaked figure she saw on the other side, and the smoky creature that rose up behind the portal, or in the portal—she couldn't be sure. How it struck the lightning in the arch and seemed to feed off it. Afterward she felt weak, too weak to defend herself, and she lost consciousness.

Taliko took over from there. Explaining his experiment to discover if the lizardlings had come from the Cave of Bones when he sensed a foul eldritch energy in the air. A summoning that confirmed they in fact had a Maker, just like him. Then his decision to settle the lizardlings deep under Point Lookout where he hoped they would be safe from the magical lure while he followed the eldritch call himself. How tracking the call had led him to the Gategrove, where he found Casey unconscious and at the mercy of the lizardling Maker—who he was shocked to discover was Nightblade, seemingly risen from the dead. Finally, Taliko recanted how Nightblade magically enhanced several lizardlings, the ensuing battle, and all that was said, leading up to Nightblade's final threat to slay them all if Casey did not open the gate for him.

"Okay," Jonas said as they neared the ranch. "I've got questions. You said 'mission' earlier; does that mean the aril sent this Nightblade creature to kill Casey? And why didn't you ask me for help when all this originally happened? And it's back from the dead? How can it be back from the dead?"

"To all ends I cannot be certain," mused Taliko. "It may be that the arrival of the unicorns somehow reawakened his dark spirit."

"Spirit?" Casey asked.

Taliko nodded. "The Maker and I erringly believed Nightblade destroyed when we confronted him. Seemingly, even though his physical body was incinerated, his consciousness survived as spectral energy. The black smoke you saw. The same cloud that trapped StarFall here."

"So…he's just a ghost? That's still good, right?" Casey asked.

"It was, for a while—fourteen years in fact," Taliko replied. "But as a result of our most recent battle, I inadvertently restored his frein enough that—"

"Enough that what?" The homesteader's eyes narrowed.

Taliko sighed. "Enough that, as Nightblade tells it…he now has enough access to his powers to perform a resurrection."

"Resurrection." Jonas shook his head in disbelief.

"Just so," Taliko said. "On this I was thinking before you arrived, and I believe he has one more task to complete before he succeeds in this endeavor."

"And that would be?" Jonas prompted.

"It is only a theory," Taliko continued. "But he confessed to be lurking by the gate while Casey worked to open it, harvesting the eldritch energy she created for himself. Then, during our battle he withdrew, letting the lizardlings carry the fight while he watched, saving his energy for something else. I believe that something is the ability to temporarily manifest his physical form."

"You think he can do that?" Jonas asked.

"I know he can." Taliko swung his damaged tail into view. "See the work of the Cree Chieftain's deadly teeth—the limb is nearly severed."

Jonas winced and grunted at the blood-caked appendage.

"But why is that so important?' Casey asked.

"Because it may be that only in physical form can he acquire the magical nourishment he needs to complete the rebirthing process."

"Magical nourishment," Jonas echoed. "Like the ice apples?"

"Just so," Taliko said.

"So, what?" Jonas asked. "We need to guard the pearlwood?"

"No," Taliko replied. "The Cree Chieftain does not dine on fruit."

"What then?" Jonas wondered.

"By consuming the only faerie creature on this side of the gate," Taliko said grimly.

Casey's eyes bulged. "He wants to eat StarFall?"

Taliko nodded gravely. "By the Nightblade's own words, so he has avowed."

Jonas saw his daughter's face set with steely defiance. How her mouth became a thin line and her hand went to the hilt of her silver long knife.

It was a look he knew, and well he should—it was the same face he saw in the mirror when the sheriff needed him on the rooftops in Storm Town.

"Right then," Jonas said. "We'll have a lot to say about that before we let that happen."

"Oh yes we will," Casey added quietly. "Yes we will."

"It is a theory only," Taliko noted. "But I fear StarFall shall confirm the truth of it. I did try to dissuade Nightblade of completing his mission, arguing its value and purpose after all this time."

"And?" Jonas prompted.

Taliko's topaz eyes connected with Casey's. "He offered our lives, if Casey would open the gate for him to go home. But to the destruction of StarFall, he would not waver."

"No way," Casey shook her head. "No deals. Not for no wolf. Not ever."

Jonas opened his mouth, not exactly sure what he was going to say but feeling as if he needed to say something, when he was interrupted by a loud rustle in the foliage up ahead.

The trio paused.

The rustle came again, then a giant lizardling wielding a crude spear in his blue claws jumped on the path from behind a thick oak tree.

"Arm yourselves," Jonas said, instinctively drawing his Colt.

A swift *sssshhhh* sounded near at hand, then Casey's blade was glinting in the sunlight beside him, but Taliko stepped forward and leveled his bo-staff horizontally across their chests.

"Wait!" he said sharply. "This is Paal."

"Paal?" Jonas asked, gun raised, eyes locked on the yellow striped creature.

"Yes," Taliko answered him. "The lizardling who resisted Nightblade's magic and helped me in the Gategrove during the battle earlier. He is a friend and leads the clan when I am away. He was instructed to return to Point Lookout, so I am surprised to find him here. It might be best if you wait here while I speak with him."

Taliko strode off toward the creature, and the pair engaged in a hissing dialogue that the humans could not understand.

"I guess the lizardlings have names now," Jonas mused. "Seems like a step in the right direction."

Casey nodded. "Seems like a lot's happened while I've been dozing at the gate. I hope StarFall is okay. Can't believe he's missing all this."

"Yeah," Jonas said. "We kind of had a fight about that."

"Fight?" Casey turned around to look him face to face. "What do you mean 'fight'?"

"Well, he wanted to come, obviously," Jonas began. "But I had just got back from Widow Dorn's place, negotiating for that filly we talked about, and I wanted him to do whatever he needed to do to…ease his pain. Told him you were *my* little girl and I would rope up whatever the problem was. He wasn't happy. Very worried about you. But I convinced him."

Casey hugged him suddenly. "Thanks. Thanks Dad. For looking out for him. I know he hasn't been about long. But he means a lot to me, and I would hate for him to be hurt on my account."

"Paal reports—" Taliko's voice came from ahead, but before he could say more, Casey detached herself from her father and moved to wrap her arms around the stocky, seven-foot-tall reptilian.

"What?" Taliko said, arms in the air, his face panicked. "Careful. Please, Casey—even my skin can damage you."

"It's a hug," Casey informed him. "To say thank you. I know you're tough, but I see how hurt you are; I see that tail all smashed up. Thank you, for saving me. It couldn't have been easy."

"It wasn't," Taliko said simply. "But I do not deserve your kindness. I have neglected my duties. Had I—"

"You certainly did!" the dam broke suddenly on Jonas's emotions. "You were supposed to be out there watching over her!"

Taliko lowered his head as Jonas thundered on. "'Stead you're messing around with those lizardlings! We're you're family! Not them!"

"Stop it." Casey raised her voice. "Stop talking about me like I'm not here. We all thought the grove was safe. Even you. Even StarFall."

Jonas shook his head from side to side, glaring at Taliko.

"If it's anyone's fault," Casey huffed, "it's mine. I've been training, but I didn't know what to expect. Now I do. Next time, I'll be ready."

"Next time? There isn't gonna be…" Jonas's voice broke, and the veteran quickly whirled away. A moment passed, then several, before a deep, cleansing breath shook his entire frame.

The silence lingered on until Taliko broke it.

"Another engagement awaits."

"Engagement?" Jonas's head snapped around.

Taliko nodded. "Against my wishes, Paal has been scouting the area for signs of Nightblade. In the process he found your track and followed it back to your dwelling to determine if Nightblade waited to ambush you there. The Cree Chieftain does not wait for you, but two human males have since arrived. Paal says they appear nonthreatening, but he is unsure of the nature of human actions and cannot be certain."

Jonas nodded, and with the battlefield acumen instilled in him by the horrors of the Civil War, abruptly prioritized the needs of the moment over his emotions.

"Okay. Let's play this casual. We don't want to tip our hand about any of this. Casey and I will double back and come out through the orchard." To Casey he said, "When we do, I want you to head into the barn to check on StarFall and stay there until I deal with whoever is on our doorstep."

Casey nodded, and Jonas turned to Taliko. "You and…and Paal here, keep to the tree line until you can see the coast is clear. Don't go and disappear again! We need to finish talking about this. Plan our next move. Deal with this Cree creature. Get StarFall home and be done with this business."

"On this we agree," Taliko said.

Back inside the grove, a shadow detached itself from the trees, startling all the birds back into the branches.

Devoid of endless avian chatter, dusk fell in the circle with an eerie silence. The spectral wolf strode to the pond and sat. Finally, as if fearing what he might find, the Cree Chieftain looked down into the crystal-clear water, and found fiery green eyes flickering back at him.

Green. Not red.

Green, the symbol of life. Not red, the herald of death.

Then there was his fur, once thick and black, now thin and scarred with flecks of gray. Perhaps he was still healing. But Nightblade suspected otherwise.

Suspected something was wrong.

His frein had been empowered beyond anything he could remember. Perhaps not how he'd planned, but just as he'd planned nonetheless. Now he just needed to feed from the juvenile to be completely reborn, a task his newly acquired alien frein would enable him to accomplish easily.

His hunter's heart should be soaring. But it was not.

Instead he felt…

Nightblade searched for the word until he found it: soulless.

Devoid of hate and rage.

Long minutes trickled by, their gait muddied and warped by the strange energy roiling within him to seem like days.

Maybe it was days, or just hours, perhaps minutes.

Had he just been sleeping? No matter.

Think. Plan.

The witch had used aspects of jevaling magic that were unknown to him to create Taliko, imbuing him with a powerful sonic thunderclap. In their first battle, the attack had been brutally painful. But this time, instead of pummeling or scattering his cloud form, it had done just the opposite, invigorating his spectral being. Restoring his frein with an undefined energy, just as it must have done for the aril witch all those years ago.

But how?

The laws of nature deemed what happened to be utterly impossible.

Light could not power the dark, and the dark could not power the light.

Nightblade rose and stalked about the oval. Thinking, trying to solve the puzzle. Eventually, he found himself on dais and paused to regard the gate.

Soulless or not, there was no doubt his brethren needed him and Nightblade desperately wanted to get home to them. There was only one way to do that.

In his spectral form, only Taliko could hurt him. More correctly, only his thunderclap and his accursed bo-staff could hurt him. But in the physical form he needed to attack the unicorn, the dreaded silver that the humans wielded could painfully drain his frein until he was powerless once more.

Swollen as he was now, Nightblade felt he was beyond those fears, and so he had offered Taliko and the humans a bargain.

Another trick.

Taliko had been close to the truth when he wondered why the Cree Chieftain had come to Earther himself. The fact was, he did not need the girl to get home. Nightblade didn't need anyone. As one of the Timeless, he was blessed with the ability to hunt prey and return home through any gate he pleased.

It was the single most valuable secret of the entire Cree Nation. A secret he guarded by coercing the aril into opening gates for him when needed and using hidden gates the aril were unaware of when required.

Fortunately, though traversing the Trailway required his physical form, his spectral essence was more than enough to guide and trick the witchling into thinking she had finally accomplished the task herself.

Taliko would warn the others of his threats now, and using the unicorn as bait, they would set up a trap for him. A trap he would stride into blithely. When his enemies struck, Nightblade would teach them the futility of trying to capture a shadow drifter.

He had to strike fast.

Once the battle began, he needed several bites of the unicorn before they filled him with silver. Then he would be whole, his frein self-sustaining—and the enemies arrayed against him would perish as easily as the deer and the rabbit.

Fangs painted, he would go home at last, victorious.

Still, something bothered him about what Taliko had said, about the bargain expiring. In that the shell warrior was correct; it had been years since he first arrived. Though chances were slim that something had befallen his ally, any variable in fulfillment should be eliminated as it arose. The stakes were simply too high to leave anything to chance.

Fortunately, his aril conspirator had given him a way to communicate. A hidden set of rune stones near the gate that would activate a magic mirror. The original intention had been to use it to confirm the kill.

Now that the final moves were in motion and he had finally regained control over his physical aspect (required to operate the mirror) it seemed wise to make contact and ensure that everything was as it should be.

Nightblade burned away a small ember of his new frein to bring forth his physical form; having revealed his continued existence at last, the time for secrecy had passed.

And the time for fear had arrived.

Long he howled at the setting sun, and to every animal within hearing distance, it was a declaration—*I am the Nightblade, and Thunder Peak belongs to me.*

The wolves of the mountain howled back to him, paying their respects, and among them there were no challengers.

Finally, he circled the reflecting pool, touching his paw to cleverly concealed rune stones hidden in each of the four stump chairs. Then he sat down to wait.

Without warning he was set upon by exhaustion, likely an aftereffect of being imprisoned in his incorporeal form for so long.

No matter.

With no idea how long it would take his ally to respond, he could trust his senses to wake him to any spontaneous eldritch flares or disturbances in the grove.

Stalking to the edge of the glade, Nightblade disappeared into the tightly woven pine needle branches just out of sight of the clearing and lay down to rest.

Content as he was that victory was as close as it had ever been, he was asleep in moments.

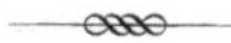

Jonas put his hand on Casey's shoulder, pausing them before they came in sight of the house.

"Sorry about losing my temper," he said. "It's been quite a week for us."

"It has." Casey agreed without looking at him.

Jonas nodded sullenly and blew his cheeks out. "I've had a knot in my stomach since this unicorn business got started. Carrying all these secrets around and now they all come out. You sure you're okay?"

Casey glanced around at the apple trees whose branches were as much her home as the ranch house, then nodded. "Things are different. Some of it's even scary, but I think, knowing about you and Mom now…I thought maybe I wanted to be a lady marshal. Because of what I thought happened. To get even. But that's all gone now. Now I can just be me. And that feels good."

Jonas smiled. "Your mother would be glad. Told me more than once she had many friends among the Apache—"

The howl-shriek of the Cree Chieftain tore across the face of Thunder Peak, startling what seemed like every living thing for miles around.

"That doesn't sound good," Jonas said, looking back the way they had come.

"No, it doesn't." Casey shuddered. "You think that's him? That must be him. The thing Taliko was talking about. The dead-not-dead wolf thing that made the lizardlings and wants to kill us all."

"That's him."

"Nightblade," Casey said timidly.

"Nightblade," Jonas repeated. "Good scary name for a monster."

"Yeah." Casey smiled shyly.

"Hey," Jonas said, drawing her gaze up to his own—a curious gleam in his brown eyes shone down at her for a long moment and Casey squinted back at the sparkle in puzzlement. "When I get rid of our company, first thing I want you to do is put on your gun belt and load up with the silver bullets I gave you. And you wear it everywhere you go from now on until this is over. Make sure you have at least a couple of your knives too, at all times."

Casey stared at him blankly, and Jonas nodded. "That's right. This is me telling you to belt up."

Casey raised her chin and quietly nodded.

"Not the reaction I was expecting. What is it?" Jonas asked.

"I'm not sure," Casey admitted. "I know things now, maybe. And what I know now makes me wish I didn't have to belt up." Then she laughed. "Crazy, right? Get me a seat next to Hickory."

"Not at all," her father said, placing his arm around her and giving her a squeeze. "In fact, it tells me you're getting a good sense of what it means to live under this crazy mountain…and the best way forward, is for you to decide when and where to belt up."

Casey exhaled loudly and nodded again.

"Thanks Dad."

They began walking again, and Jonas steered them out of the grove beside the barn. The sunthorns had come out, their wings humming pleasantly in the woods around them, and for a moment, it seemed as if there was nothing unusual about their lives. As if they had gone back in time to the day before Casey had first seen a unicorn.

Then Jonas saw there were two men who had made themselves comfortable on the porch swing and immediately recognized the dappled gray of one of their horses.

"Seems the sheriff has come to visit."

"Ugh," Casey grumbled. "Not now. You can't leave now."

"Mighty strange he be here himself," Jonas mused out loud. "See to StarFall in the barn, and stay there until I come fetch you. Understand?"

"Yes, Dad."

Jonas took no chances. Removing his pistol and holding it at his side, he skirted the property from twenty-five feet and peeked around the front of the house.

The two men in the swing were rocking and speaking softly. One of them was indeed the sheriff, and aided by his aril moccasins, Jonas walked up behind them quietly.

When he reached the porch, Jonas said, “Hello, sheriff,” prompting both men to jump to their feet, hands on the butt of their firearms.

“Damnation, Jonas Tamm!” the sheriff said, removing his hat and wiping his brow. “You trying to get shot?”

“Not in particular, sheriff,” Jonas replied easily, glancing at the stranger with him. “Not ’spectin’ a social call either. And I’m guessing you’re not here to trade for some apples.”

“No,” said the sheriff. “But maybe you can spare a couple while we talk. If we’re alone, that is.” With that the sheriff leaned closer. “Might be best if your daughter don’t hear this.”

“All right. Come inside. How’s the shoulder?”

“Doc says I’ll be fine,” Tanner answered, following Jonas into the house. “By the way, I also wanted you to meet my new deputy, this is Craig Towson.”

Jonas nodded. “New name in Storm Town.”

Sheriff nodded. “Just come in. Balt-more was it?”

“That’s right,” the man said, extending his hand to Jonas. “Heard ’bout you. Pleasure.”

Jonas was already extending his hand and started. “How’s that?”

Craig’s eyebrows shuffled up and down, “Oh, you know, in town. The sheriff’s right-hand man.”

“You must be mistaken,” Jonas said, peering sharply into the other man’s eyes. “I’m not a deputy. Just a rancher.”

“Right,” Craig began, “the rancher who helps…” Apparently seeing something in Jonas’s face, he let it go and raised his hands. “Hey, I’m not lookin’ for any trouble. I just got here. There was some saloon-talk about the gunfight with the Red Ridge Riders. Man on the roof who helps the sheriff on the tough ones. Man on the roof who doesn't miss. That's all. I'm looking for work. The sheriff give me some. Now we're out here. Just putting two and two together."

"Funny thing about the saloons in Storm Town…" Jonas began, but when he stopped to let his words sink in, the sheriff stepped into his pause.

"Jonas," the sheriff said smoothly, "I gave him the same speech I gave you. Same one I give everyone. You know my policy. Don't matter where you been, if you made it here, you get a chance till you prove otherwise. Don't let loose lips in the saloon get things off to a rough start."

Jonas nodded and smiled tightly. "Right then. Welcome to Thunder Peak. You've got big boots to fill."

Craig exhaled and smiled back. "Thanks. I'll do the best I can."

Jonas led them to the kitchen area and tossed each of them an apple from a basket on the table.

Craig bit into his, and his eyes sparkled. "Jingo-dang!" he exclaimed. "Sheriff told me about these apples on the way over, but this…" He took another bite and swallowed. "This is unbelievable."

Jonas smiled. "Help yourself to another when you're done."

"In this canyon your apples are like money, Jonas," the sheriff said. "People trade them for everything, even drinks at Sticky Jacks."

"Do they?" Jonas was genuinely surprised. "I didn't know that."

"Jacob Miller hired Mills a few times to escort him down the shaft to meet up with his trading partners at Itza Chu Landing," the sheriff continued. "They come from New Mexico. They pay him lots, then trade over to Texas, up to Colorado and even Wyoming to make it back and more. Miller paid Mills handsome like, to keep his mouth shut. But he told me, and he's gone now, so…might be time you renegotiate some of your prices. You do plenty for our town, and I hate to see you taken advantage of."

Jonas waved a hand. "I have plenty for everyone."

Sheriff Tanner nodded, and both of them regarded Craig for a moment, enjoying his apple as much as anyone ever had anything in their life. Finally, Jonas turned back to Tanner. "So, what's this about sheriff?"

The sheriff looked at him and gave a weary sigh. "Those thieving Red Ridge rustlers are still camped out by the back door. Ain't been up to much since the Aces High, but they ain't moved off yet neither."

At mention of the Aces High, Jonas glanced at Craig and found it hard to tell if he was simply enjoying his apple or studying his home. *Damn*, he thought. *So worried about them seeing StarFall I brought them inside when I should have just taken them around the grounds for a stroll.*

"Worse yet, I think we got more of them too."

Jonas flicked his eyes back to the sheriff. "More?"

Tanner nodded. "More. Most accounts had them camped around two or three campfires. But I went into the hills myself two nights back with my spyglass."

"And?" Jonas prompted, still more curious than worried.

"Five campfires. Hard to be sure, I didn't want to get too close and be spotted, but it's a good bet the gang's doubled."

"At least," Jonas frowned. "You want me to take a look?"

Jonas, usually tight lipped about the War Between the States, had once mentioned being a scout, so Sheriff Tanner appeared relieved by the offer of his expertise. "I'd be obliged if you would, Jonas."

Jonas nodded, and Tanner added, "Plus, we got this fool business of the Full Moon Ride heading our way. You heard about that yet?"

Jonas shrugged. "Some kind of horse race?"

"Endurance race." Tanner nodded. "Starting and finishing on our doorstep. Down the shaft to Itza Chu Station and back. What are they thinking? They're places all over this valley that's sacred ground to the Apache, the Comanche, and every other Indian in the territory. They tolerate our little town, but the hubbub of a big spectacle is bound to get a war council started."

Tanner shook his head from side to side. "Minute Geronimo or some other chief hears about this, they'll be blood. Course just the fool idea is luring everyone within two hundred miles to Storm Town. And more bad than good too, I'd wager. Following the news, looking to catch on with anyone and willing to do anything. Could be the sort what's swelling the ranks of the Ridge Gang."

Jonas used the reflective moment to casually cast his eyes toward Craig again, and it seemed to him that the deputy paused midbite when his eyes alit on Liberty's carving. *Seven bells to glory*, he thought, chastising himself.

"Planning a raid on the stake money you think?" Jonas wondered out loud.

"Could be." Tanner shook his head. "Could be the whole town! There's just too darn many new faces in the canyon to get a clear idea of what anyone's about. Saloons are both bursting, and new wagons come every day dropping stakes and pitching tents. So I been playing my part, keeping my eyes open, and making the rounds, spreading the word about this Full Moon Ride so our residents and townsfolk can spare themselves the irritation of strangers till this is all over if that's how they please."

Tanner looked Jonas in the eye, and Jonas nodded back his understanding.

"Meantime"—Tanner didn't miss a beat—"I've recruited about everyone to keep their Peacemakers handy. Course I know better than to formally try and deputize you, but if trouble comes calling—"

"You can count on me, sheriff." Jonas cut him off. "As always."

"Much obliged, Jonas," the sheriff said.

Tanner looked at Craig and saw two cores on the table already. "Best we be heading off before Craig here eats your whole orchard."

"And we still need to swing by Widow Dorn's place on the way back," Craig added.

Tanner waved off his deputy. "Fool is smitten with that schoolteacher, Widow Dorn's niece, Ms. Sherwood. Don't embarrass me, Craig. I gave you that star, and I can take it away."

"Wouldn't think of it, sheriff," Craig said with a smile.

Jonas showed them out. Craig exited first, and Jonas placed his hand gently on Tanner's shoulder to stop him in the doorway. "I'll get back to you soon as I can about what I find in the hills; might be a few days."

"Race is some ten days off. Day of the full moon, next Tuesday. We know what we're up against before then; that'll help. Old as most of us are now, when Storm Town folk know what needs doing, they done it all before and ain't afraid to do it again. So that gang tries anything, we'll get the old church bell ringing and they'll be in for a fight. Still, I got a bad feeling about this one, Jonas. Bad feeling ever since we lost Mills."

Jonas nodded. "We'll get it sorted, sheriff. We always do."

Sheriff Tanner nodded and swung up on his horse. Then, with a tip of his hat, he and Craig were riding off toward the Dorn residence.

Watching them go, Jonas was surprised to discover just how much the mention of Alice Sherwood and Craig's interest in her was bothering him.

Then he turned his mind to the sheriff. Tanner was nervous. That much was obvious.

Another long howl shattered the stillness, and Jonas saw Tanner and Towson throw a nervous look toward Thunder Peak.

Watching them spur their mounts away, Jonas shook his head from side to side. He would do what he could for Sheriff Tanner and his Storm Town neighbors, but at the moment he had much bigger problems.

Once the sheriff and his new deputy departed, Jonas set off for the barn and found Casey, Taliko, and StarFall waiting for him inside.

"Trouble in town, Dad?"

Jonas nodded. "Gang that caused trouble the other day is still up in the hills. Might or might not have something to do with some crazy horse race being set up."

The moment he said it, Jonas wished he hadn't.

"Horse race?" Casey asked, glancing at StarFall.

Jonas chuckled. "Yeah. Endurance ride down the shaft from Storm Town to the old Butterfield Mail Station at Itza Chu Landing. Crazy stuff. Don't even think about it."

Casey nodded, then said, "StarFall and I could win that race easily."

"I have no doubt." Jonas agreed. "But he's not just a horse in our barn like Rebel, is he? You'd have to ask him if he wants to do it. And right now, with him bleeding from the head, barely able to stand and needing to get back so his horn can grow, I think he just wants to go home."

"I know," Casey sighed. "I'm just saying. I'm a great rider, and he's the fastest thing on four legs, probably in the whole country."

"Right then," Jonas said, changing the subject. "Taliko, I apologize for losing my wits. I just—"

"Say no more, friend Jonas." Taliko interrupted him. "You were not wrong. Nightblade is a cunning foe who has now tricked us all. I for one must endeavor to be at my best to be sure it does not happen again."

"Good advice for us all." Jonas nodded. "Now, have you two had a chance to talk to StarFall about Nightblade? What can he tell us?"

"I self-arrived just before you," Taliko replied, shaking his head no.

Jonas nodded again and got comfortable on a hay bale.

"I'll ask him," Casey said, turning to the unicorn. "Have you ever heard of something called a Nightblade?"

StarFall backed up a step. "Nightblade?"

"So you've heard of him then?"

"Of course. He and his pack are the enemy of every woodland being in

Leutia," StarFall replied through Casey. "Countless have perished under his tooth and claw. How is it you know of him?"

"He's here," Casey informed the unicorn.

"Here!" StarFall's forelegs rose in the air.

Casey nodded. "Here for me, apparently."

StarFall reared again, eyes wide. "The treachery of the aril knows no end. To conspire with the Nightblade is unthinkable amongst every herd."

"It gets worse," Casey said, and StarFall tilted his head in query. "Before he can get on with his mission to kill me, Taliko thinks he needs to eat you first."

StarFall stepped back farther, head swaying left and right, taking his time before answering.

"This would explain why Nightblade has not been seen in Leutia for over a decade. His people, the Cree, have retreated so deep into the woods that many seers speculate he perished in some manner."

Casey nodded. "Well, he was killed, sort of, by my mom and Taliko. Only he didn't stay dead, and now he's back and he's hungry."

StarFall nodded and said, "After my Wrivening I would need to eat regularly from trees and shrubs like the snowbark, the tree you call pearlwood, to keep my frein strong. So after all this time being trapped without any faerie creatures to sate his vicious appetite, it makes sense that he needs to…hunt the first faerie being he sees to regain his strength." StarFall's eyes widened in realization. "He it must have been that was the black cloud that exiled me here!"

"And the dark influence that spurs the stinging insects that plague your travels," added Taliko.

"The source of my fears reveals itself," StarFall observed. "But my fear falls woefully short of its true identity." Then, looking at the shell warrior, he shook his head in disbelief. "I find the advisement of your victory nothing short of incredulous. Back home, a tale of Nightblade's defeat is a story unwritten. All honor to you and your Maker, Taliko," StarFall dipped his head respectfully. "I am in awe of your bravery, and would care to hear the details of the battle without delay."

"Me too," said Jonas.

Taliko twirled his staff once and drove it into the ground with a thud. "And so I begin the telling of the Maker and the Merciless."

"Merciless?" Casey asked, eye wide.

Taliko nodded, "Nightblade, Merciless. To the Maker, such were the names of the enemy."

Casey mumbled, "Suits him fine, I reckon. Just fine."

Taliko stared at the floor a moment, then looked up at Jonas and began. "At the Maker's behest, I told you that she tasked me with bringing Casey through the portal and to deliver her safely to your nest."

Jonas nodded for him to continue but Casey said, "Hold it. In, not out on the porch. In. How did you get me *in* without breaking down the door?"

"Hoof dust?" StarFall asked.

"The tale goes just so," Taliko replied.

"Hoof dust?" Casey asked.

"Unicorns are forever free," said StarFall. "Magic born with the ability to open any lock. Such is the legacy of SkyMajesty, the mother of all faerie steeds. It is a rarely given gift, but as a reward for great services, unicorns sometimes allow mages to take a splinter from their hoof to use as an ingredient for magic spells and substances that will open doors and other locks."

"SkyMajesty," Casey said dreamily.

"Her sacrifice gave birth to both unicorns and pegasai," StarFall explained. "A story for another time perhaps."

"A story for another time, definitely," Casey said.

All eyes fell back on Taliko, signaling him to continue. "Much like the story you told Casey of how she came into your care Jonas, the tale of my bringing

Casey into yours was also a falsehood to forestall questions. In truth, friend Jonas, how Casey came to be delivered into your nest, I cannot say. The first thing I remember is the Maker's eyes. Green and soft, like newborn river leaves in the sun.

She said to me, 'I regret that like many before you, you are raised into a world of violence. However, your purpose is born of love. The purpose is everlasting. That purpose is to aid my *lolien* in raising and protecting our daughter Seyca from all dangers. And so your name shall be... *Taliko*, whose meaning is guardian. Rest now, my shell warrior, but just for a little while. Our time is short. The merciless one will strike soon, and you have much to learn if we are to succeed.'"

"Wait, wait." Casey interrupted him, shaking her head from side to side. "Say-ka?"

"Seyca." Jonas nodded. "The name your mother gave you. At least that's what *he* said when we first met." Jonas pointed at Taliko. "That part's probably true though, since it's also stitched into the gold blanket you came in."

"Well, where did Casey come from then?"

"Never heard tell of anyone named Seyca." Jonas shrugged. "So I shuffled the letters like cards until they turned into Casey. Made up the stagecoach story—instead of questions I got sympathy."

Casey closed her eyes and shook her head, trying to reconcile this latest revelation with the rapidly changing world she had woke up in barely a week ago.

Her father added, "I wasn't pulling the long bow when I said I knew a secret about your parents, was I?"

Casey looked at her father, and he flashed a winsome smile at her.

"*A* secret?" she said, shaking her head again. "Book of secrets more like. And the book of Jonas got more mysteries than Matthew, Mark, Luke, and John put together."

Jonas absorbed that for a second, then burst into an uncontrollable fit of laughter.

"Ah, Casey," he wheezed after several knee slaps and belly aches. "I needed that. And if that's the truth, I'm the gladder for it. Mysteries just might be the harvest of a life worth living."

"If you say so." Casey rolled her eyes.

"I do." Jonas's tone turned serious. "And now you've got some mysteries of your own to protect. Nash and Savannah came 'round today. You can't go telling them or anyone else about StarFall or any of this."

"I understand," she said.

After exchanging nods with her father, Casey turned to Taliko and said, "On the subject of mysteries, how could you understand what Mom said the moment you were born?"

Taliko directed his gaze at Casey. "I was born from an egg, a common turtle—until the Maker, your mother, raised me into what I am now with jevaling magic. If the spell is powerful enough, the raised is granted what is called Maker's speech. It is simply woven into the magic from the beginning. The lizardlings did not have Maker's speech in their initial form, but then Nightblade jevaled some of them a second time, making them stronger, smarter, and imbuing them with Maker's speech, and so I can communicate with them more easily now.

"While I rested, the Maker cast additional spells that imbued me with unique abilities, including the knowledge of your language. During my waking hours, education and combat training aided by spells cast with the assistance of frein stones, went on for several days before—"

StarFall whinnied, and Taliko looked toward the glistening ebony steed. "Indeed. There were five. Each as big as Casey's fist."

Jonas slapped his knees and strode around the barn.

Taliko swiveled his head in the homesteader's direction and said, "And you wonder why the offspring is so impatient."

"Offspring?" Casey grimaced. "Ick. Let's not use that again if we don't have to."

"Red, gold, green, blue, and purple." Taliko turned back to the unicorn. "I know this for certain because they remain in my possession. Even now they are in my nest, casting light, and in the case of the green, even heat."

StarFall whinnied again and looked at Casey, who stepped over to stroke his neck.

Taliko nodded and said, "The day of reckoning broke while the Maker was meditating, and I practiced with my staff. Quite suddenly she opened her eyes and said, 'The merciless one is here. Time now, Taliko; fate offers us two choices and two choices only. Victory or destruction. Seize your fate with bravery, whilst I face mine without remorse or regret."

Jonas sighed quietly, looking at the floor and rubbing his eyes.

After a short pause, Taliko continued, "We raced through the woods and intercepted the enemy on his way—"

StarFall abruptly cantered forward, ears twitching.

Then Taliko stood, and seeing that both of their eyes were on the barn door, Jonas rose into a combat crouch and drew his pistol.

"What is it?" the rancher asked, as Casey came to her feet beside him, long knife in hand. "Nightblade?"

StarFall moved closer to the doors and whinnied loudly.

"He says they're here," Casey whispered.

"They?" Jonas echoed.

"The unicorns." Casey lowered her blade.

Then a wide smile overtook her face and she turned toward her father. "Dad!" she gushed. "It's the unicorns! They're here! Once we tell them about Nightblade, I'm sure they'll help us defeat him. Then they'll bring StarFall home and everything will be all right!"

Emotions soaring on bright new wings of relief and delight, Casey stamped a foot into the ground and twirled on her toes with outstretched arms.

"I knew this was going to have a happy ending," she exclaimed. "I just knew it!"

Jonas exhaled, straightened up and slid his pistol back in the holster.

He exhaled again, louder this time. Then, lips parting in a bright grin, the former soldier turned toward StarFall, ready to ask if he should open the doors.

Something about the steed's bearing stopped him.

Three heartbeats came and went. Then his eyes were back on the barn door. His steady right hand back on the Colt's grip.

If the unicorns had come to help him, why did StarFall look so nervous?

THE TAMM CHRONICLES

WILL CONTINUE

IN

BOOK II

THE GALLOPING GHOST

TAMM CHRONICLES

GLOSSARY

ALICE SHERWOOD: Storm Town's schoolteacher.

ANCIENTS: Fabled race of builders who created the Tyndryn Trailway and explored the worlds they connected.

ARIL: Inhabits of Leutia. As a nation, known for selfishly monopolizing and monetizing their control over the Tyndryn Trailway, placing them at the heart of discord across the entire realm. Aril are recognizable by their slender builds, angular features and light colored hair.

BACKDOOR: Steep mountain defile through which one can enter Itza Chu Canyon from the southeast.

CASEY TAMM: Daughter of rancher Jonas Tamm.

CONNIE DORN: Owner of the Double D Ranch.

CREE: A superior wolf inhabitant of Leutia. As a nation, presided over by Nightblade and feared by all for their sudden raids and ruthlessness. Cree wolves are unmistakable for their size, saber teeth and great cunning.

EARTHER: Leutian translation for the human realm known as Earth.

FREIN: See Appendix A

GATEGROVE: Clearing deep inside Itza Chu Canyon where a Tyndryn Gate is hidden.

ITZA CHU CANYON: Secluded, temperate crevasse hidden in the shadow of Thunder Peak Mountain. Terrifying tales of strange creatures, ghosts and inexplicable weather patterns from inside the canyon have driven pioneers and travelers to shun the area, but rumors persist there exists a haven for outlaws and other fugitives deep in the valley for those brave enough to find it.

ITZA CHU STATION: Butterfield Mail post that has fallen into disuse except as an occasional stage stop for weary or lost travelers.

JACOB MILLER: Proprietor of Storm Town's General Store

JEVALING: Magical process by which lower reptiles, insects, birds, fish, and animals can be enhanced into beings with greater intelligence, size and strength.

JONAS TAMM: Rancher. Civil War Veteran.

LEUTIA: Homerealm of the aril, unicorns and Cree.

NIGHTBLADE: Chieftain of the Cree Nation. Often referred to in poems and songs as the Merciless and/or the Wolf Lord.

POINT LOOKOUT: Mysterious lighthouse shaped tower deep inside Itza Chu Canyon that has fallen into ruin.

RED RIDGE RIDERS: Gang of rustlers and outlaws terrorizing the Arizona Territory.

RIELL: Aril Sentinel. Known on Earther as Mae.

SHAFT: Long winding trail that is the primary route between Storm Town and the desert outside Itza Chu Canyon.

STARFALL: Juvenile Unicorn. Scion of the Sapphire Woods.

STORM TOWN: Unruly epicenter of commerce and socializing tucked deep inside Itza Chu Canyon. Populated mostly by retired outlaws, gunslingers, grifters and con artists.

TALIKO: Casey Tamm's woodland guardian.

THUNDER PEAK: Dark spire in the Arizona Territory perched at the south-western edge of the Chiricahua Mountains. Widely regarded as haunted because of its unpredictable weather, strange wildlife, and long history of ghost sightings.

TYNDRYN TRAILWAY: Network of magical portals that can teleport individuals from one place to another over great distances and even between worlds.

UNICORN: Magical steeds recognizable from horses by the horns on their foreheads. The hoof folk are often denoted by their intelligence, isolationist tendencies and rigid aloofness.

WALT TANNER: Storm Town's Sheriff. Friend of Jonas Tamm.

WINSTON, NASH and SAVANNAH: Brother and sister. Casey's friends who live on a nearby farm.

TAMM CHRONICLES

APPENDIX

FREIN

Frein is the measure of an individual's intrinsic ability to summon and manipulate eldritch energy for use in spell casting. Among spell weavers this innate reserve is commonly referred to as the *well.* There are two types of frein: Golden and Shadow. In most cases golden frein is harnessed by beings of harmonious alignments and shadow frein by those with darker tendencies.

Personal Frein Capacity varies from race to race and individual to individual. Spell weavers enhance their powers by learning how to strengthen and maximize their abilities through training and research. It is generally believed to be impossible to increase one's personal frein capacity by any noticeable degree because the time required to master the feat is typically beyond the lifespan of the known races. The possible exception to this rule, naturally, are dragons who are extremely long lived. However, dragon ecology is closely guarded by the species and no official studies have been made. There have been rare cases of individuals working together to temporarily increase their frein capacity as a group, but every recorded incident has resulted in the death of at least one of the spell weavers involved. Rarer still, is the use of powerful magic items to increase frein capacity. Beyond being highly dangerous and very time consuming to craft, said items are reportedly limited to one use, making them unique. Currently there are no known items with this power in existence.

Personal frein is recharged with physical rest, but each type also has its own way to speed recovery. Golden frein can be restored by eating or drinking from blessed sources including, but not limited to, water, fruits, berries, and herbs. Shadow frein predators can consume faerie beings (those that have at least trace amounts of frein) to reinvigorate themselves with blood magic. Rumors of viscous "blood pools" hidden around the realm and used by evil dragons, the Cree, crimson griffons and other "monsters" to restore their black wells have persisted since the beginning of time but have never been substantiated. It is widely documented that when journeying to magic dead realms the traveler must return home to recharge or bring appropriate sustenance on the journey to recover expended frein.

The seeding of magic dead realms with blessed orchards has met with very little success. The most promising of these was Earther, but travel to the volatile realm has been extremely limited since the *Black Powder Massacre*. As a result of that incident, the Tyndryn Trailway remains closed to any new seeding expeditions. The abrupt decision to close the Trailway to new expeditions instantly evolved into a political flashpoint between numerous nations that persists to this day, and many sages agree that it has but one inevitable outcome: War.

ACKNOWLEDGEMENTS

Writing and publishing a novel requires endless inspiration and support. For that, first and foremost I must thank my lovely wife, Macie. She keeps the gates of my imagination open. Just as important, the example she sets with her personal work ethic resolutely urges me through the difficult aspects of the publishing process.

And of course, you Mom. Your genuine enthusiasm for all my stories was always, and shall always be, my reserve tank. I was so lucky to have you when you were here, and I know the memories of your tireless support and confidence will ever propel me to each new horizon. I hope you are proud.

First Rounders are essential early readers that help pinpoint details that can go so very wrong. In that regard Thunder Peak was enhanced by two premium picks: Dawn Patane and John San Pietro.

Finding the right art is always tough. Thunder Peak was fortunate to find Abhimanyu Artbot to add finishing touches to the front cover.

I have since learned that acquiring cover art and uploading it for publication are totally different things. A great many thanks to Renaissance Man Rick Varone, for taming a host of unruly pixels and coaxing them to bookend a legible spine for Thunder Peak.

I have endeavored to be as accurate as possible regarding history, culture and the daily routines of the Old West. Any mistakes, oversights or unintended slights that may have slipped through are on me, and for them, I apologize.

CPSIA information can be obtained
at www.ICGtesting.com
Printed in the USA
LVHW022217150622
721376LV00004B/335